P. M. Hubbard and The Murder Room

>>> This title is part of The Murder Room, our series dedicated to making available out-of-print or hard-to-find titles by classic crime writers.

Crime fiction has always held up a mirror to society. The Victorians were fascinated by sensational murder and the emerging science of detection; now we are obsessed with the forensic detail of violent death. And no other genre has so captivated and enthralled readers.

Vast troves of classic crime writing have for a long time been unavailable to all but the most dedicated frequenters of second-hand bookshops. The advent of digital publishing means that we are now able to bring you the backlists of a huge range of titles by classic and contemporary crime writers, some of which have been out of print for decades.

From the genteel amateur private eyes of the Golden Age and the femmes fatales of pulp fiction, to the morally ambiguous hard-boiled detectives of mid twentieth-century America and their descendants who walk our twenty-first century streets, The Murder Room has it all. **>>>**

The Murder Room
Where Criminal Minds Me

themurderroom.com

P. M. Hubbard (1910–1980)

Praised by critics for his clean prose style, characterization, and the strong sense of place in his novels, Philip Maitland Hubbard was born in Reading, in Berkshire and brought up in Guernsey, in the Channel Islands. He was educated at Oxford, where he won the Newdigate Prize for English verse in 1933. From 1934 until its disbandment in 1947 he served with the Indian Civil Service. On his return to England he worked for the British Council, eventually retiring to work as a freelance writer. He contributed to a number of publications, including *Punch*, and wrote 16 novels for adults as well as two children's books. He lived in Dorset and Scotland, and many of his novels draw on his interest in and knowledge of rural pursuits and folk religion.

By P. M. Hubbard

Flush as May (1963)
Picture of Millie (1964)
A Hive of Glass (1965)
The Tower (1967)
The Custom of the Country (1968)
Cold Waters (1969)
High Tide (1970)
The Dancing Man (1971)
The Whisper in the Glen (1972)
A Rooted Sorrow (1973)
A Thirsty Evil (1974)
The Graveyard (1975)
The Causeway (1976)
The Quiet River (1978)
Kill Claudio (1979)

A Rooted Sorrow

P. M. Hubbard

An Orion book

Copyright © Caroline Dumonteil, Owain Rhys Phillips and Maria
Marcela Appleby Gomez 1978, 2013

The right of P. M. Hubbard to be identified as the author of this work
has been asserted in accordance with the Copyright, Designs and Patents
Act 1988.

This edition published by
The Orion Publishing Group Ltd
Orion House
5 Upper St Martin's Lane
London WC2H 9EA

An Hachette UK company
A CIP catalogue record for this book is available from the British Library

ISBN 978 1 4719 0081 5

www.orionbooks.co.uk

To George and Margaret Hardinge,
with gratitude and affection

I

He recognised the cottage instantly and in detail, but it did not seem at all familiar. It was like a cottage seen in a picture, or perhaps more in a film, where the camera had tracked all round it and up and down inside it, leaving him still sitting, detached, in front of the screen. The whole place was obviously the place that had been on his mind, almost night and day, for the last five years, but now that he had come back to it, it was less real than the one he had had on his mind. This immediately raised the question whether he had done any good to come, but he was committed to it now. He got out, opened the gate and drove the car up the steep curving drive to its garage at the back of the building.

Not its garage really. It was not the same car. The same model, only the colour was different, but it was another car that had stood here five years ago. As he got out, he had a momentary, breathless conviction that the driver was different, too, a different person. Like the cottage, superficially recognisable, but not really the same. It would be fine if it was true, only it would make nonsense of the whole thing. He took the key off its nail on the wall of the outside lavatory and unlocked the back door. It swung in freely for a bit, stuck for a moment where the bottom caught the unevenness of the cement floor and then, when he pushed it over this, swung on faster and came up with a bump against the side of the china cupboard. He had not consciously remembered any of this, but he did not run into the door when it stuck. On the contrary, his hand was on the handle, ready to give it the extra push when it needed it, lifting it a little, and then to hold it back so that it did not hit the cupboard hard enough to do any harm. With the door open, he remembered the smell at once.

It was odd what houses smelt of. It could not be the people, or even the things the people did in them, because over the years the people changed, and different people did different things, but the house, in between, went on smelling the same. You could overlay the smell of a house temporarily with smells of your own, and almost certainly, as with all smells, you could get to overlook it, but you could not exorcise it altogether, and when you come back, even after quite a short absence, there it was, pleasant or unpleasant according to its associations in your mind, but the same smell.

It was the smell that got him over his uncertainty and persuaded him that he really was back, the same person back to the same place. He remembered, with a rush, a whole number of things that had happened when he had smelt that smell before. He had thought about them all at intervals over the years, but not the smell that went with them, and now he had that, he could no longer doubt that he was the person they had happened to. He stood for a moment in the middle of the kitchen, looking round. Then he turned and went to get his things out of the car. There was no need to go through into the other rooms until he had the things to put in them. There was nothing he needed to see. He knew what there was there.

He was going out for almost the last load of stuff from the car when he met Mrs. Basset in the doorway. She must have been watching for the car, as she always had. She could not see it turn in off the road, because the gate and most of the drive were hidden by the hill, but she could see it go across the front of the cottage. There was just the moment or two between its appearance over the shoulder of the drive and its disappearance round the back of the house, but if she knew it was coming, she would not miss it. Her cottage faced south at the bottom of the hill just as his faced south at the top, and like most people who live in cottages, she spent more time looking out at the back than she did looking out at the front. She could find any number of useful things to do and still not miss the car, once she knew it was coming. It was Mrs. Basset he had spent more time thinking about than anything else, but when he saw her, she was as unfamiliar as the cottage.

She had in fact changed, but then so she would have. People did change more than places or things, even in five years, even people like Mrs. Basset. He could not have said what the physical changes in her were, but it was not the physical changes that mattered. It was her state of mind he had had in his head all these years, and her state of mind, as she stood there in the doorway facing him, was quite unfamiliar. She looked at him with a mild interest, just strong enough to bring her up the hill as soon as she saw the car, but not really amounting to curiosity. There even seemed to be some amusement in it. Whatever it was, it did not worry her, nor did he. He had expected to worry her, and had expected to feel bad about it, merely as a natural extension of what he had been feeling all these years. He was disconcerted, but did not have time to feel glad of the change.

She said, 'Well, Mr. Hurst. I saw the car and thought I'd come up. You got everything you want? You'll be glad to be back.'

'Yes, thank you, Mrs. Basset.' He meant that he had everything he wanted, not that he was glad to be back. He had not meant to be, and could not let himself agree that he was. 'You're looking very well,' he said. She was, too; he could see it now. There was more flesh on her face, and she looked smoother and a better colour. He had remembered her eyes staring, but now they did not stare.

She said, 'Oh yes, thank you, I always keep well.' She seemed surprised that he should have mentioned it, as if it was hardly worth mentioning. 'You're looking well yourself,' she said.

He said, 'I'm all right.' It was the least he could say, but he did not really mean it. It was because so little was well with him that he had come. 'How's Lizz?' he said.

'Elizabeth? She's fine. Works in Frantham now. She's a secretary at Morris's, the solicitors. Quite grown up, of course. You'll see.'

He nodded. 'She would be, of course.' He looked at her, but there was still no strain in her face. She waited placidly for what he was going to ask. 'And Jack?' he said.

She said, 'We don't hear from Jack.'

He nodded again, but this time he lowered his eyes. 'I'm sorry,' he said.

'Well, I don't know.' He looked at her again, and found she was almost smiling. 'I reckon he's better away. Better for him, too, I mean. I don't worry about him.' She saw his face change and said, 'He didn't really fit in here. It wasn't the place for him, do you think?'

'Perhaps not. So long as you don't worry.'

She shook her head. She was quite certain. 'I don't worry,' she said. She was watching him now. 'And Miss Garstin's married,' she said. 'Mrs. Richards, she is, now.'

'Is she? That's good.' He gave her back certainty for certainty, and she accepted it, smiling.

'Well,' she said, 'If there's nothing —'

'No,' he said, 'don't worry. It was nice of you to come up. I'll look in presently.'

'Any time. You'll find us all much the same.' She turned and went off round the house, and after a moment he too went out to the car. So Christabel was married, to someone

4

called Richards. He did not remember anyone called Richards round here. Maybe they did not live round here, but Mrs. Basset had sounded as if they did, as if Christabel was still part of the place. Christabel was married, and Lizz was a grown-up secretary called Elizabeth, and Mrs. Basset was a placid, smooth woman, whose eyes no longer stared, and who found nothing to worry about. He would find them all much the same, she had said, but that could not be right, from what she had said. Had she forgotten or had he?

He took the rest of the things out of the car and put them down on the gravel while he shut the car up. The sun was out now, not at all hot but very bright, and the little wood behind the cottage was in new leaf. It looked thicker than he remembered it, so grown together that you could hardly get into it. From here the trees did not look very much taller, but he supposed they must be. There was no wind at all, and even the leaves did not move. There were birds singing among the trees, but he could not see them. It was all very peaceful. He picked the things up off the gravel and carried them across to the back door and into the kitchen. He left everything where it was and went across to the door into the sitting-room. He did not mind the smell of the house, there was nothing wrong with it, but the sooner he got the windows open, the better.

The rest of the house was like the kitchen, perfectly predictable, but not really familiar. He stopped trying to put things away and sat down in his usual chair to think. To say he was not the same as the person who had sat here five years ago was attractive, but it would not really do. He remembered the place and what had happened there, and you cannot remember what has happened to someone else. He had spent a lot of time remembering. His memory constituted a large part of the continuity of experience that bridged the gap between then and now, and the experience itself was real enough. It was only that, now that he had finally made himself go back over the bridge, he found this sort of gap at the farther end. The things he remembered, now that he came back to them, were somehow less real than his memory of them. It was his memory that had brought him back, but it had not landed him quite where he expected.

It followed that there were still decisions to be made. It had taken him five years to decide to come back, and he had assumed that, once he had decided, the rest would follow. Now he was not so sure. What had looked inevitable to his memory seemed arguable to his present experience. He had not done with his memory, but he must consider the facts. For a start, he must see Christabel. He got up from the chair. It struck a little cold as he sat in it, and had the smell of the house. He went on with his unpacking.

When he had finished, he went out of the front gate and down the path towards Mrs. Basset's cottage. He looked at his watch. It was still too early for Lizz to be home from Frantham. He did not want to see Lizz just yet. Not that she was likely to be important in herself, but she might be a distraction. He went right down the path into the road, and then turned and went into Mrs. Basset's front gate. Later in the year the front door would be standing open, but it was not warm enough for that yet. He went up the flagged path and knocked on the door.

A man opened it. He was a big smiling man in his shirt-sleeves and seemed very much at home. The man said, 'Hullo, Mr. Hurst,' and they smiled at each other. The man knew him and he knew the man, only he could not for the life of him remember his name or who he was. The man saw his difficulty and did not hold it against him. He said, 'You don't remember me. John Merrow.'

6

'Of course. I do remember you, but I couldn't put a name to you. You live down Furzehill Lane.'

The man still smiled, but he shook his head. 'Not now,' he said. 'I live here. My lease fell in there, and if it hadn't been the lease, it would have been the roof. And Mrs. Basset had the room. Do you want to see her?'

'Well – yes, but nothing special. She told me to look in.'

'That's right.' He stood back from the door. 'Come in,' he said. 'I'll call her.'

They went into the front living-room and Merrow opened the door at the bottom of the staircase and called up it. 'Amy,' he said, 'there's Mr. Hurst here to see you.'

Mrs. Basset said something he could not catch, and a moment later she came down the stairs, moving lightly for a woman of her age. She shut the door of the staircase behind her and stood there, looking from one to the other of them and smiling slightly. She said, 'You remember Mr. Hurst, John?'

Merrow was still smiling, too. He had his hands in his pockets. Everybody was very easy and pleasant. ' 'Course I remember him,' he said. 'He couldn't put a name to me, but he remembered me, all right. And where I lived.'

He looked at Mrs. Basset and Hurst wondered whether she would find it necessary to explain Merrow's presence in the house, as he had done, but she did not. 'That's right, he would,' she said.

'I tell you one person I can't remember,' Hurst said, 'Richards. You said Christabel – Miss Garstin – had married a Mr. Richards, but I couldn't place him. Did I know him?'

Her eyes flicked sideways to Merrow and came back to his again. They were both still smiling. 'No,' she said, 'no, you wouldn't have known him. After your time, he was. It was Mr. Martin in your time.'

7

'Martin?' he said. 'I don't – the only Martin I remember was the parson in Frantham. But —'

'That's right. Well, he went – oh, three or four years back, and then Mr. Richards came.'

There was a moment's complete silence. Then Hurst said, 'Do you mean Miss Garstin married the parson?'

'She did, yes.' There was laughter held in on both sides of him now, waiting to see what he would do before it showed itself.

He did not laugh, because he did not feel like laughing, but he could not bring himself not to show that he knew what they were waiting to laugh at. He allowed himself a small turned-in smile and a shake of the head. 'Well,' he said. 'I shouldn't have expected that, I must say. But so long as she's happy —' He was elaborately decent about it, and the laughter never came.

Mrs. Basset put on a serious, social face. 'Oh, I think so,' she said. 'A nice man, he is. I think they get on very well. Of course, we don't see much of her now. Not like when she was living here.'

'No. No, you wouldn't. What happened to the house, then?'

'Oh, she sold it when she married Mr. Richards. It was hers, of course, after her mother died. Some people called Barnes have got it now. Not like it used to be, though, when old Mrs. Garstin was alive and Miss Christabel was there. Quiet people, Mr. and Mrs. Barnes, and they haven't got a family, or not at home, anyway.'

Hurst nodded. He felt no interest in the Barneses whatever. He said, 'You've looked after the cottage beautifully, Mrs. Basset. You'd never think it had been empty all this time. Everything's just as I left it.'

'Well,' she said, 'it's a dry little place up there. Gets all the sun in front, and the trees keep most of the rain off behind. You'll be looking after it yourself now, same as you used to?'

'Oh, well, yes, if that's all right with you. I'm used to looking after myself.'

'Oh yes, I've got plenty to do without that. I still go in to Mrs. Barnes, like I used to to Mrs. Garstin.'

'That's fine, then.' He moved towards the door.

Mrs. Basset said, 'You won't stay and see Elizabeth? She'll be back soon. She's wanting to see you.'

'I mustn't stay now, no. But I want to see her, of course. Can't I still call her Lizz? That's how I always think of her.'

Mrs. Basset laughed. 'You can try,' she said. 'She may take it from you. She won't from us. Better wait till you see her.'

Hurst laughed too. 'All right,' he said. 'Wait till I see her. But I must go now.' He said his good-byes and went out into the quiet, chilly sunshine. Outside the gate he turned right and started walking steadily along the road. He did not think he would go as far as Frantham now, but he wanted exercise, and there was a lot to think about.

He walked a few hundred yards and then changed his mind again. If he stayed on the road, he would meet Lizz coming home on the bus. At least, he assumed she came on the bus, but however she came, this was the way she would come. Then she would see him from the bus, but the bus would not stop, and she would recognise him, because he had not changed much, but he might not see her, and even if he did, he might not recognise her, not just going past in the bus. He did not want that. He wanted to have a good look at her when they did meet, if possible even before they met. He turned off the road, climbed a field gate and set himself to walk up in a circle through the fields, so as to come at the cottage from the far side. Even Mrs. Basset

9

would not see him come in then. They would see his lights later, and know he was at home, but they would not have seen him come in. That gave him a sense of privacy, and privacy was very important.

The bus went past on the road below when he was well up the hill. He stood and watched it for a moment. Then he turned and went on with his walk.

II

The tapping on the door startled him, but even before he was out of his chair, he made up his mind that it must be Lizz tapping. It came again while he was on his way to the door, and this time he had no doubt at all. The impatience was characteristic, and the light, quick, repeated taps were like her, too, even though he could not remember her ever tapping on his door before. She would be using the tips of her fingers, typist's fingers perhaps, not knocking with the knuckle as most people did. He found himself agitated, but even before he had the door open, he recognised a quality of pleasure in his agitation. He lifted the latch, almost deliberately took a breath and then swung the door right back, so that the light fell fully on her as she stood outside.

She was wearing some sort of cloak, with a hood pulled up over her head, so that all he could see of her was her face and one hand holding the cloak together in front. The cloak and hood shone with drops of water. He had not known it was raining. There was still no wind at all, and the rain fell very quietly in the silence. Her eyes were still very wide and blue, but they were a woman's eyes. Even the hand was a woman's hand, calculated and cared for, not the unconscious hand of childhood. For a moment they stood there, taking each other in. Then he said, 'Hullo, Lizz,' and she said, 'Hullo, Mike,' almost simultaneously, and he stood back from the threshold.

'Come in,' he said.

'Do you mind?' The voice was surprisingly deep, not husky, but full-throated. She came a step into the doorway, and then turned and swung the cloak off her and shook the beaded water into the damp darkness outside. She was wearing a plain dark dress, with long sleeves and a touch of white at the neck and wrists. Office dress, he thought. He wondered if she generally changed when she came in, but this evening had kept her dress on to go visiting. He hoped so. That would be like her. She had always had a sense of occasion, even as a child. She dropped the cloak over a chair by the door and came on into the room. He shut the door and followed her. She was only a little taller than he remembered, but her whole body had filled out. Physically she was very much Mrs. Basset's child, and none the worse for that. Only the face and eyes were different. She turned again, and for quite a long time they stood there, looking each other up and down in a friendly, deliberate way. He was still agitated, but there was no embarrassment in it at all.

He said, 'Of course I don't mind. I wanted to see you. I never thought you'd come up, though.'

'Why not? I always used to.'

He considered this. 'I know that,' he said. 'I suppose I thought you wouldn't feel the same.' But he knew this was not true. It was not that he had expected her not to come; it was that, now she had come, he was surprised she had. With part of his mind he was not even very pleased. He did not want her to feel the same about him, because he felt very differently about her. But he could not have known he was going to feel so differently about her, not until he had opened the door and seen her standing there.

She shook her head. She had stopped smiling and was suddenly very much in earnest. 'I feel just the same about you,' she said. 'You don't mind, do you?'

He gave it up. He smiled and held out his hands to her. 'Lizz, Lizz,' he said. 'Of course I don't mind,' and she put

12

her hands in his and stood there looking up at him. The doubts were on her side now.

'Still friends, then?' she said.

He nodded. 'Come on,' he said, 'sit down and tell me everything.'

She sat on the chair opposite him. In the old days she had used to flop back into it with her arms dangling and her legs all over the place. Now she sat sedately, a little sideways and knees together. She said, 'Your Christabel's married.'

'I know. Your mother told me. She wasn't mine, anyway.'

'Wasn't she? I was never quite sure. I knew you were desperate for her, but I was never sure how far you'd got. Even when you went off, I still wasn't sure. Only I thought you'd gone because of her, one way or the other. God, how I hated that woman.'

She sat staring into the fire, but when he said nothing, because he did not know what to say, she looked up and saw the way he was looking at her. 'It's all right,' she said, 'I wasn't jealous, not really. But I was afraid what she might do to you. And she did – I mean, it was because of her you went, wasn't it?'

He hesitated, and this time she did not look at him. She simply sat there, waiting for him to answer. He thought, good God, if I boggle at this, what is the good of my coming at all? 'Well, yes,' he said, 'in a way, it was.'

She nodded. 'She never wanted you,' she said. 'Not as a permanency. She liked having you hanging around, of course. She couldn't have too much of that. Or too many of them, if it comes to that. She didn't mind who it was. Even brother Jack she had a go at. Mrs. Basset's boy down at the cottage, and her Mrs. Garstin's daughter up at the house. But Jack was tougher than you were, quite a bit. It took

13

more than Christabel to play him up. He was off and away even before you were. Only I don't think that was her doing.'

He looked at her long and fixedly. 'How do you know, Lizz?' he said.

'Know what? About Christabel and Jack? Oh – things I noticed. I knew Jack very well, you know, even though he never talked much.'

He said, 'I never knew —' and checked himself, but it was true, up to a point.

'You wouldn't,' she said. 'Trust Christabel. And Jack, if it comes to that.'

He thought. 'What about Jack?' he said. 'Your mother says you don't hear from him.'

'Jack's got away,' she said. She was quite matter-of-fact about it, as Mrs. Basset had been. 'It's better, really. That's what he always wanted. And things are easier without him, let's face it, much easier.'

'For you, do you mean?'

'Well, for all of us. There was never any peace while he was around. And now John's got Jack's room, which keeps Mum happy. And anyway, John's much more use in the house than Jack ever was.'

He said, 'Jack wasn't the only tough one in your family, Lizz.'

'Well,' she said, 'Dad was tough. You never knew him. Anyway, I'm not tough. Just realistic. I like people to be happy if it can be managed. And Jack couldn't stand John, not at any price. They couldn't stand each other. There was no chance of having John in while Jack was around, and Mum was always sweet on him. He's nice, too, you know.'

'Will they marry, do you think?'

She shrugged. 'I shouldn't think so. I think John's got a wife somewhere, or had. I suppose they could manage it if

14

they wanted to. But why worry?'

'And Christabel's married the parson?'

'Yes.' She looked at him, trying to feel her way behind the question, and he looked at her with no expression on his face at all, until she gave it up. 'Mum thinks it's funny,' she said. 'Well, I suppose it is, in a way. But he's quite something, Mr. Richards is, parson or no parson. I think a lot of women would marry him if they had the chance. And it's all quite fair and above-board. She doesn't play the parson's wife at all, and I don't think he wants her to. He just carries on the way he used to before he was married. I mean, so far as the parish is concerned. It seems to work all right.'

'I see. All the same, I wonder why she married him. She could have taken her pick, too, you know, pretty well.'

'All right, I grant you that. I don't reckon there was anything personal in it, on her side, I mean. But there wasn't much choice, either. She'd have taken the squire if she could, but there wasn't a squire available, so she took the parson. An attractive parson, mind you, and pretty stinking rich, by all accounts. And she hadn't much of her own, you see – that was the point. The old lady had an income from a trust, but not much of it went to Christabel when she died. It may be fun playing around when you've got an indulgent old dragon to keep house for you, but not such fun when you've got a big old house on your hands and nothing to run it on. The house was Mrs. Garstin's, and came to her. So what do you do? You sell the house and stuff to give yourself a lump of capital, and then find someone else to look after you.'

Hurst said, 'You're very well informed.'

She shrugged. 'I work for Morris's,' she said. 'They're the only solicitors hereabouts.'

He said, 'You're a dangerous woman, Lizz.' He said it smiling, but she looked at him perfectly seriously.

'Only when I'm interested,' she said. 'Most of our business leaves me cold. But I've been interested in Christabel for a long time now.'

She stared into the fire, and he sat there looking at her and taking her in. Dark hair, pale skin, blue eyes with dark lashes, plain dark dress, good plain shoes, pretty, compact, very sure of herself. He said, 'I think I'll call you Elizabeth, may I?'

She looked up at him sharply. 'All right,' she said, 'Why?'

'Well – you're not Lizz any more, are you?'

She was looking into the fire again. 'Not really, no,' she said. 'Lizz died a year or two back. I don't miss her much.'

'No? I wonder whether I shall?'

'You shouldn't,' she said. 'Anyhow, missing her won't bring her back.'

'No, all right.' He thought for a bit. 'I want to see Christabel,' he said.

'Of course. No harm in that. Get her out of your system. You'll get no change from her, I warn you. She's playing it very careful nowadays.'

He said, 'I've told you, she's not in my system. Anyway, perhaps Christabel's dead too, and there's only Mrs. Richards left.'

She lifted her face and looked at him, very long and steadily. 'I don't know about dead,' she said. 'That sort never dies. But dormant, anyhow. Anyway, you go and see her. You won't wake her in a hurry.' She stood up, neatly and quickly, all in one movement. 'I'd better be going,' she said.

'All right.' He got up too and went for her cloak. He held it out for her, and she came and turned her back to him while he put it round her shoulders. Just for a moment he held her like that, with his fingers feeling the firm warmth of her upper arms. Then he dropped his hands, and she turned and faced him. She said, 'Good-bye for now then, Mike,' and he said, 'Good-bye, Elizabeth,' and her hands came up and pulled the hood over her head.

He opened the door. It was still raining very gently outside, and very dark. He said, 'Haven't you got a torch or something?'

She said, 'No, no, I don't need one,' and went straight out into the darkness. For a moment he held the door open, watching her feet stepping quickly and lightly under the bottom of the cloak. Then he shut the door and went back to his chair.

The room still smelt faintly of Elizabeth. He had not noticed any scent about her, not even when he had put her cloak round her shoulders. She had not seemed the sort of person who would use it, or not much of it, anyway. But now that she was no longer here, he knew there was a scent in the room which had not been here before, lingering like the new and powerful attraction he was half resentfully aware of. Lizz had been his friend, the only real friend he had had in the place, the only person he had felt safe and at peace with. But now Lizz was dead, and there was this new, formidable Elizabeth in her place. He did not feel safe with her at all. Elizabeth had offered him her friendship and he had accepted it, but they had both known it was not as simple as that.

And it was not only Lizz that was dead. The distraught, watchful Mrs. Basset was dead, too, and Christabel, who had harried him to the brink of endurance and at last over it, Christabel was dead and had left only Mrs. Richards, the rich parson's wife. The whole small world he had known here was dead, and he was the only survivor. Or perhaps he was the one that was dead, and it was the rest who had gone on living. He had come back to exorcize a ghost he could no longer live with, but it could be that he himself was the ghost, and had come back uselessly to haunt a world that had been managing to live very well without him. His mind oscillated between the familiar determination of despair and the unfamiliar, almost unwelcome, intimations of a new hope, until the only thing left tolerable to him was physical activity. He got up and went to the door and opened it.

The rain had stopped, and there was a breeze moving in the trees behind the house. He could even feel it on his face. He shut the door behind him and stood there, letting his eyes get accustomed to the darkness. The cloud was moving, too. There was no moon, but already there was a scattering of stars, and before long the night would be clear. He went back into the house and put on a coat. Then he went out again, leaving the lights burning behind the curtains in the sitting-room, and picked his way cautiously down the path to the road. The tarmac showed in a faint luminous ribbon between the dark of the hedges. He turned left and began walking steadily. He knew where he was going now, and ten minutes later he saw the lights of the house standing up to the left above the road.

He did not know anything about the Barneses, but they did not sound the sort of people who would be out and about at this time of night. The gates were still painted white, and when he came to them, he turned in and went quietly up the gravel drive under the overhanging trees. He knew all about going up the drive quietly, just as he had known all about opening the back door of the cottage, without consciously remembering either. He could not have gone quietly up the drive as often as he had opened his back door, but it had meant more to him, and the impression had been proportionately deep. When he came to the end of the trees, he stood, still in the black darkness under them, and looked across the sloping stretch of lawn to the front of the house. There were lights in two of the ground-floor windows, but the curtains were thick and closely drawn. The upstairs windows were all dark, and it was impossible to tell whether they were curtained or not. Not even the quiet Barneses would have gone to bed at this hour, but he suspected they kept the house pretty well sealed. The first thing they would have done was to install central heating, because that was the first thing anybody did nowadays when they moved into an old house, and Mrs. Garstin had clung to the splendid, laborious tradition of open fires. He did not think anyone would see him if he moved across the grass. He himself could see well enough now, but to anyone coming from a lit room the night was still very dark. He walked, slowly but steadily, straight across the smooth turf towards the far end of the house.

When he came to the window, he saw that the curtains were not drawn, but the room inside was dark. It was a corner room, with an ordinary window in front and a french window at the side, and by putting his face close to the glass he could just make out the shapes of the furniture. It was quite different, of course. Christabel's big book-case had gone from the side of the door and there were no pictures on the walls and as far as he could see no flowers. The big sofa had gone from in front of the fireplace. He wondered whether she had it with her in her new room at the Frantham vicarage. Perhaps she had not got her own sitting-room there, but from what he knew of her he thought she would have. Besides, if she was in the vicarage but not wholly of it, as Elizabeth had suggested, she would need something of the sort, and from what he remembered of it from the outside, there would be plenty of rooms to spare. But perhaps, after all, she no longer wanted the sofa.

Now that he had come right back to the heart of his mystery, he was conscious of that curious, unexpected numbness that he had experienced at intervals ever since his arrival. He shivered suddenly as he stood there, but the shiver was one of pure physical chill, because the wind was getting up, blowing over the wet country, and the glass of the window was cold against his forehead and nose. He took his face away from it and stood back, utterly at a loss, but still somehow satisfied. There was nothing more he wanted here. He turned and went back the way he had come, straight across the grass to the trees at the bend of the drive. It was time he went home.

III

It would not be Christabel who opened the door, he was
sure of that. To open the door to any casual caller at the
vicarage would be to involve yourself, willy-nilly, in parish
business, and she was not doing that. The woman who in
fact opened it was someone he had certainly never seen before, and not even, judging by her voice, a local. He supposed she might be someone the vicar had had before his
marriage, and perhaps brought with him to Frantham. As a
well-to-do bachelor with a whole-time job, he would have
had a housekeeper of some sort, and this might well be her.
Her age and manner made it possible. There would be local
dailies, but they would hardly run to a living-in maid as
well, not these days, not in Frantham vicarage. It looked as
if Christabel was indeed, as Elizabeth had said, getting herself looked after. He wondered how she and the housekeeper got on, but he thought she would carry it off all
right. Her manners were pretty enough if she set her mind
to it.

He said, 'Mrs. Richards?' and the woman looked at him
with just that touch of inscrutable speculation he would
have expected.

She said, 'Yes, will you come in? I'll just see if Mrs.
Richards is free. Who shall I say it is?'

He went into the hall, and she shut the door behind him.
'Mr. Hurst,' he said. She nodded as if the name meant
nothing to her, and went off down a side passage, leaving
him standing there. He was sure he was right about her. It
was all perfectly businesslike and polite, but there was none

of the formal civility of even the superior servant. The woman would not eat with them, but she would have her own sitting-room and be an equal member of a triumvirate. He had never been inside the vicarage in Mr. Martin's day, and could make no comparisons, but the hall made a very pleasant impression. Not like a vicarage at all, he thought, and then wondered if this was a prejudiced view.

A beautiful long-case clock ticked majestically at the end of the hall, but there was no other sound in the house. The ordered silence superimposed itself on his inward unease and left him doubtful and confused. The woman was back almost at once. She said, 'Yes, will you come? I'll show you.'

He followed her down the passage to a door which was already standing open. She said, 'Here's Mr. Hurst,' and he went in and heard her shut the door behind him. It was a small room full of sunlight. Christabel was standing with her back to the fireplace. She said, 'Hullo, Mike. I'm so glad you came. I'd heard you were back.'

He said, 'Hullo, Christabel,' and stood there, just inside the door, looking at her and the room. If it was not an exact reproduction of her room at the old house, it was very like it, and had much of the same stuff of it. The sofa was back against the wall, but it was the same sofa. He had forgotten how beautiful she was, and above all, how elegant. He supposed this was because it was not in the end her beauty and elegance that you remembered about her. The lines of face and body were long and delicately drawn, and her eyes had the expression of slightly amused good humour that you see on the faces of people who have been habitually indulged but have not let it, in the ordinary sense, spoil them. He saw all this with a new and almost startled admiration precisely because he knew, at the same time, that the hold she had had over him was broken, once and for all, and could not be

22

renewed. He wondered, as you always do, about her husband, and what he saw in her and how much she let him
see. Meanwhile they stood there, smiling at each other. It
was all perfectly friendly and polite, but he wondered
whether it was not, after all, her smile that gave her away or
whether perhaps with him she did not mind if it did. But it
might be only his imagination.

She said, 'Come and sit down.' She pointed him to one
end of the sofa and sat down herself at the other. There was
plenty of space between them. 'You're not looking very
well. What's the trouble? Isn't the work going well? It
seems some time since you had a new book out.'

He found this disconcerting. Everyone else had said how
well he was looking, and he had found that disconcerting,
too, because he had not felt well. Now he was disconcerted
because he had not expected Christabel, of all people, to see
anything wrong with him, and because he knew she would
not in any case read the kind of books he wrote. 'Not very,'
he said. 'There's one on the stocks, but I have been held up
with it, in fact.'

'So you've come back here to try to get things sorted
out?'

There seemed no sense in denying this. 'In a way,' he
said, 'yes.'

'Then I hope you manage it.' It was still friendly, and
even concerned, but he was not sure that the concern was
altogether with himself. Somewhere in her mind there was a
touch of calculation. 'I wondered,' she said, 'would you like
to come and have a meal with us? I'd like you to meet
Charles. Or would you rather be left undisturbed?'

He thought about this quite deliberately, as she meant
him to think. Then he said, 'No, I don't think I want to be
left undisturbed.'

She nodded. 'Then you'll come if I ask you?'

23

'Yes, I'd like to.' What he really meant was that he was willing to, perhaps even that he thought he must, but this was not a thing you said.

She said, 'Good. I'll find a date and let you know. You're still not on the phone?'

'Not here, no. I'd rather not.'

She nodded. 'And you found everything in order?'

'Oh, yes. Mrs. Basset has looked after it beautifully.'

She nodded again. He waited for her to go on. He had never been able to do this before, and he was determined that the new position should be made clear. She said, 'The girl's grown very pretty. Smart, too. She works here in Frantham. I expect you know that?'

She was feeling her way, and he thought on what different terms he and Elizabeth had discussed her, and how curious the difference was. 'Yes,' he said. 'Yes, she told me.'

She smiled at him. 'No longer the kid sister?' she said, and he smiled back cheerfully.

'I shouldn't think so,' he said. 'Very grown up.'

She gave a little laugh, but she was no longer interested, and for quite a long time neither of them said anything or looked at each other. Then she said suddenly, 'I'm really very happy, Mike. You'll like Charles. I think he'll like you if you'll let him.'

He looked at her, and for a moment they stared at each other from their opposite ends of the long sofa. Then he smiled, though she was still serious. 'Why shouldn't I let him?' he said.

She shook her head. 'I don't know. I have a feeling you don't want to be liked, not as you used to. Do you know at all what I mean?'

'Yes,' he said, 'I think I know what you mean.' He was no longer smiling. They were both almost solemn. 'Anyway,' he said, 'I'm glad you're happy, Christabel,' but he wondered as he said it whether, as he had thought, the old Christabel was dead, or whether, as Elizabeth had said, she was only dormant. He wondered more than ever about Charles Richards.

She said suddenly, 'Mike, why did you come?'

'Do you mean here, to the vicarage?'

'Well, that too, I suppose. But I mean, why did you come back to this place at all?'

She was looking at him very direct. The dark lashes no longer drooped over the green eyes, and the eyes themselves held something that might be anger, or even apprehension. There was a new Christabel here, he thought, different from either of the two Christabels he had known before. It was a Christabel not to be easily put aside, even from his new-found position of strength. All the same, he tried. 'Well,' he said, 'it's my place. It's my cottage. I lived here quite a long time.'

'Why did you leave it, then?'

'I had to. You ought to know that.'

'Because of me?'

He had been this way before, and he gave the same answer. 'In a way, yes.'

'I'm sorry,' she said. She meant what she said, but he shook his head at her.

'Why should you be sorry?' he said. 'You're happy. You've just said so.'

'And you think you'd have prevented that if you'd stayed?'

'I might,' he said. 'Not that that's why I went, I'm not pretending it was.'

She looked away from him at last. The sun had gone in, and the room seemed suddenly much darker. 'I wonder,' she said.

For a time she said nothing, and he watched her, seeing

her beauty vividly but remotely, as through a sheet of glass. Then she said, 'You're an odd person. I think you've changed a lot, haven't you?' She looked at him again, but uncertainly.

'I was thinking the same of you,' he said.

'Is that what you came here to find out?' The question came very quickly and sharply, and there was the same concentration of emotion in her face, but he still could not tell quite what the emotion was. All the same, he found the question easy enough to answer.

He said, 'Yes, I think so.'

'You came back simply to find out?'

'No. No, that's not quite right. I came back with a purpose in mind. My purpose rested on my memory of the place and people. Well— it would, naturally. When I got here, I found that my memory was no longer necessarily valid, and that called my whole purpose in question. So I had to find out, as you say. About you, among other things. Does that make sense?'

She nodded, rather listlessly. All the force and concentration, whatever it was, seemed to have drained out of her. 'It makes sense,' she said. 'It doesn't tell me much.'

Just for a moment, and quite suddenly, he felt sorry for her. He had never felt sorry for Christabel before, and it took him a little time to recognise what he felt and wonder why he felt it. He got up and stood in front of her, holding out his hands. 'Come on,' he said. 'I'd best be going. I didn't come here to upset you. I suppose the truth is I didn't think I could.'

She put her hands in his, and he pulled her gently to her feet. 'You ask me to dinner,' he said, 'and I'll come and meet your Charles. Will you do that?'

For a moment they stood there, very closely face to face, with her hands still in his. Then she smiled at him, and he

smiled back. 'All right,' she said, and he let her hands go
and stood back from her. 'But you can upset me,' she said.
'You did, even before. Will you remember that?'

'I will,' he said. He still did not understand the implications of this. He would have to think about it, but only after
he had left her.

She said, 'Good,' and he opened the door for her and
followed her along the passage into the hall. The great clock
still ticked by the end wall, and there was still no other
sound anywhere in the house. She opened the front door
and stood aside, and he went out on to the steps in front.

'I'll hear from you, then,' he said.

'Yes. I'll ask Charles and fix a date. Good-bye till then,
Mike.'

He said, 'Good-bye, Christabel,' and turned and went
down the steps. The whole sky was covered with cloud. He
thought it might rain before he got home, and he was not
dressed for it. He went quickly down the short drive and
out into the High Street. He did not know any of the people
he saw, and he did not think any of them knew him. Half
way along the street he passed a brass plate saying Morris
and Morris, Solicitors and Commissioners for Oaths. It was
an old plate and well polished, but the windows on either
side of the door were screened, and he could not see inside.
He looked up at the dark sky and hurried on.

Whether or not Elizabeth had seen him go by, he
thought she would want to know about his meeting with
Christabel. This evening, or if not this evening one evening
soon, she would come up the path and make her little patter
of sound on his door, and when he let her in, she would
question him very directly. She would question him because that was the sort of person she now was, and because
their old friendship gave her a privileged status which he
could not deny, even if it had yet to be proved that the

friendship had survived the changes of five years in both of them. Now that he had seen her again, he did not want to talk about Christabel to Elizabeth, any more than he had wanted to talk about Elizabeth to Christabel. They were two separate and very different people, possibly opposed, though the opposition, if it was real, seemed to be conscious only on one side. He had to make up his own mind about both of them, but their relation to each other was something he was not concerned with and did not want to get involved in. Even if he knew what to think about Christabel, he did not want to tell Elizabeth what he thought; and Elizabeth was not an easy person not to tell things to. It was a complication that galled him, because it intruded on the privacy of his own dilemma.

The rain held off until he reached Mrs. Basset's. From here he could go up the direct path to the front of his own cottage or take the side road that led past his gate and drive on the other side of the hill. He did not want to do either, or not yet. He did not want to go home yet at all, and he was near enough now to get there without getting too wet if the rain did start. He walked straight on along the main road until he came to the Barneses' house. It was so dark now that some of the ground-floor lights were on, but the corner room at the eastern end of the front was unlit. It was as though the room was dead, and its spirit had passed to that other room at the Frantham vicarage—a south-east corner room, too, now he came to think of it. Perhaps the room was not dead but haunted, as he himself was haunted, by things that had happened there, and the Barneses found it difficult to use, as it was said people did find haunted rooms. But he was playing with the idea, going round and round the thing and making it more complicated than it was, because this took his mind away from what hurt it and what it had got to come to grips with. It was another temptation away from reality, like the temptation to believe himself a different person from the one who had been here five years ago.

He was standing there in the road, staring blankly in at what was now the Barneses' house, when it occurred to him to think what sort of a picture he would make if anyone came along the road, or if the Barneses themselves looked out and saw him standing there. This would not do. You only lost privacy by drawing attention to yourself. He turned and started back towards the cottage, and at the same moment the rain began to fall. It fell heavily on the instant, as if the water really had been piling up in the steadily darkening clouds until it had got too heavy and the bottom had fallen out of them. Even from where he was, he was going to get wet before he reached home. He started to run, swearing at himself as he ran, not because he was getting wet, but because he was behaving so foolishly.

He ran up the path to the front of the cottage, gasping for breath now, with his head bent and his feet slipping on the wet scoured surface of the path. The front door did not stick as the back door did. He flung it open and dived into the sitting-room, so that his head crossed the threshold before any of the rest of him. Then at last he straightened up, turned and shut the door.

He took his jacket off and shook it, but he was not really so wet after all. The house was completely quiet and very dark. He could just hear the rain falling steadily on the roof, but there was no other sound anywhere. He hung his jacket over the back of a chair and went through into the kitchen. Unlike Mrs. Basset, he did not spend more time in the kitchen than he could help, because from here there was nothing to see but the little wood. It stood there now under the rain, quite motionless, but with every twig and leaf drooped to let the water run off it. It bowed its head, as he had done, but it did not have to run, because it had not made the ridiculous human mistake of covering itself with an absorbent outer covering. The water ran off it and fell through it and soaked into the earth at its feet. But you could not see the earth from here, because the wood was too thickly grown.

He stopped looking at the wood and put a kettle on to make himself some tea.

IV

He slept at the back because it was more private. In front
the upstairs windows commanded long views. They were
too high for anyone to be able to see into, but the windows
themselves were visible from a long way off, and he did not
like feeling that everybody for miles around could see
whether or not the curtains were drawn and when the lights
went on and off. At the back the windows looked directly on
to and over the top of the wood, but with the trees growing
as they were you would not be able to see over them much
longer. West of the wood there was nothing but the long
slope of fields. East of it his own small hill fell sharply to the
side road, but the road was not much used, and there were
no houses on it for another mile or more. If he wanted to
have his light on and read at all hours of the night, there
was no one to wonder why he did not sleep like everyone
else, and if he wanted to lie late in the morning with his
curtains drawn, he need not feel guilty about it. At this time
of the year the birds sang in the wood from the first grey of
daylight, but he did not mind the birds. The noise they
made only emphasised the silence, and they gave him a feeling of security, because if they were there, no one else was.
All the same, it was no good lying too long and listening to
them, not once you were fairly awake and knew you could
not get to sleep again. It was better to get up and start doing
things, even if no one else knew whether you were up or
not.

He got out of bed and put on his dressing-gown and slippers. He did not know what time it was, because he always

left his watch downstairs when he went to bed. The time was a thing you were better without at night. It was broad daylight, and the birds had been singing for a long time. The curtains were drawn across the windows, but behind them the windows were open. He went across and flung the curtains back, and saw John Merrow standing at the back of the house. He stood a little uncertainly, as if he had seen no signs of life in the place and was wondering whether to knock at the door or go away again. The curtains moved silently on plastic runners, and he did not hear them when Hurst pulled them back. He still stood there, looking out over the fields past the western side of the wood. It was a fine clear morning, and the sun, away on the other side of the house, was getting quite high. Merrow looked like a man who had been up some time. Hurst did not want to talk to him like this, in his dressing-gown and slippers, but better that than let him go away with nothing to think about but the fact that he had found no one awake. He lent out of the window and said, 'Hullo, John. Sorry, I must have overslept. I was up late last night.' This was not exactly true, but it was a standard part of the act.

Merrow turned and looked up at him. He looked a little startled and guilty, but quite good-natured about it. He said, 'Oh, hullo, Mr. Hurst. I didn't want to disturb you. I was just going away, as a matter of fact. I didn't see anybody about.'

'Oh, don't go away. I'm just going to come down and make myself some tea. Come in and have a cup with me.'

Merrow said, 'Well —,' and took a step towards the back door, and Hurst pulled his head in and went downstairs to let him in. The dressing-gown was sober enough, in fact, and Merrow looked at it sympathetically, as if he really believed Hurst had been working late at his writing. If it had been flowered silk, he might have had his doubts.

32

Hurst led the way into the sitting-room. The curtains were not drawn here, and the room looked just as it did in the day-time. He always opened them at night, after he had turned the lights out, so that in the morning no one could tell whether he was up or not. He said, 'Sit down, John, and I'll put the kettle on. It doesn't take long. It's one of the quick ones.' He went back into the kitchen, leaving the door between them open. He filled the kettle and switched it on. Then he put the cups and things on a tray, and ran hot water out of the tap into the teapot to warm it. The kettle was singing already. Out of the corner of his eye he watched Merrow through the open door of the sitting-room. He had not sat down, but was standing by one of the front windows, looking down towards the back of Mrs. Basset's cottage. When Hurst brought the tray in, he turned, smiling. He was a big man, and looked very strong, but all his movements and expressions were unexpectedly gentle.

He said, 'It's nice the view you've got here. I've been up with Amy sometimes when she's come up for the cleaning. I've always liked it. It's a pretty place altogether.'

Hurst was busy with the tea-things. 'Yes?' he said. 'Yes, it is nice.' He made Merrow sit down at last and handed him his tea. Then he took his own cup and sat down opposite him. There was yellow, early-morning sunlight in the room, and in it the two men sat sipping their tea and looking at each other.

'Well,' Merrow said at last, 'it's what I came about, really. I hope you won't mind. Just a sort of try-on.' He smiled to neutralise the suggestion of guile in what he said.

Hurst said, 'Yes?' again, and waited. He had no fear of Merrow at all. It was himself he was afraid of, and of the way he might react to whatever Merrow said.

Merrow took his time. He drank his tea slowly, not looking at Hurst, as if he was thinking how to say what he had in his mind. Then he put his cup down on the table beside his chair. 'Well,' he said, 'you've been away a long time. The truth is, I've been wondering what you intended doing with the place.' He gave him another of his quick, disarming smiles and looked away again, moving his head from side to side, as a sort of visual demonstration of his mental hesitation. 'I mean,' he said, 'you've got your own place, I suppose, up nearer London, and I was wondering if you were thinking of keeping this one on.' He gave Hurst a quick look, not smiling this time, and went on before he could say anything. 'Only if you were thinking of selling,' he said, 'I wondered if you'd let me make you an offer, before you put it on the market, like. I've got a bit of money saved, and I reckon I could give you a fair price.' He looked at Hurst again. 'That's if you were thinking of selling at all,' he said.

Hurst had put his cup down and taken a hold on himself, but he was unprepared for the gush of extraordinary gratitude and affection that welled up in him. Just for a moment he let himself believe that he could lift the burden he carried off his own neck and lay it on this big, kindly man, but it was no more than a moment. Because he had taken a hold on himself, and his grip was by now very practiced and assured, his face did not change. He looked merely thoughtful; not pleased, certainly not offended, merely thoughtful. He said, 'I see.'

Merrow waited for him to go on, but when he did not, he got out a little more of what was in his mind. It occurred to Hurst that he had considered the thing a lot, and had got all his words ready, so that now, once the thing was launched, he spoke without his earlier hesitations. 'You see,' he said, 'I've always lived round here, ever since I could remember, and I'm fond of the place. And if you was to go, I thought perhaps you'd rather someone like me had the place. I mean, someone who'd let things be, and not go mucking about with it, and building on to the house and cutting down trees and all that. And so far as I'm concerned, well, I'd like a place of my own, that's the truth, if I could still be here, like.'

Hurst said the first thing that came into his head, and it surprised him a little, but was something he really wanted to know. He said, 'What does Mrs. Basset say?' He had never called her Amy. It did not seem appropriate.

Just for a second Merrow hesitated, as if he too was surprised at the question. Then he said, 'I haven't asked her.'

Hurst nodded, and Merrow went on, as if he had been taken a bit out of his course, and felt further explanations were needed. 'Well, you see,' he said, 'I'd be near enough, here, and of course I'd have more room here. I can look after myself, same as you can, and I expect she'd give me a hand with it. But I reckoned it would be better, one way and another. And as I say, I thought you might be glad of it, that's if you'd got no further use for the place.'

Hurst had got over his upset now and was really thinking. He knew beyond any doubt what it was he wanted, even though it was something he had never consciously wanted before, only he did not know at all whether it was possible. He thought on, his face its accustomed blank, until Merrow said, 'I hope you don't mind my asking you. It'd be up to you, of course.'

Hurst lifted his head and smiled at him, and Merrow smiled back, and the curious affection and trust there was between them came suddenly out into the open. 'I don't mind a bit,' Hurst said. 'Only the truth is, I haven't really thought about it, and it needs some thinking about.'

'That's right, I understand that. I'd want you to think about it, of course. Only I thought if you was to know how I stood on the thing, you could take your time, like, and not do anything on the sudden.'

Hurst said, 'That's very nice of you, John.' He said it because he meant it, and it only occurred to him afterwards that it might have seemed an odd thing to say.

Merrow at least seemed to see nothing odd in it. He said, 'Well, just so as we understand each other. I shan't say anything to anyone, of course.'

'No, all right.' Hurst was thinking again, so that for the moment he had almost forgotten that Merrow was there. Merrow had changed things, given him something entirely fresh to think about, but the moment he had done this, Merrow himself had receded from the front of his mind. He was unused to thinking about other people at all, except as elements in his own situation. Once they had taken their place there, that was what they mainly represented, and to deal with them personally, apart from that, seemed an unnecessary complication. The feeling he suddenly had for Merrow, and Merrow's own suggestion, had changed the situation, but it was still the situation he was concerned with. All the same, the feeling was there, and it roused him out of his thinking about the situation into a sense of the need to do the right thing by the man. He looked at him and smiled. 'Have another cup of tea, John,' he said. 'I'm very glad you came.'

When he looked up, Merrow was watching him, perhaps a little concerned, but his face relaxed when he saw him smile, and he smiled back. 'Then I'm glad, too,' he said. 'It took some doing, and that's a fact.' He picked up his cup and got up and brought it over to the tray. 'I'd like another, if I may,' he said. 'I generally do, this time of the morning.'

That brought Hurst back to his original predicament, only now it did not seem to matter. He poured out second cups for both of them. 'To tell the truth,' he said, 'I don't know what time it is.'

It was Merrow who now felt the oddness of this, and he looked at Hurst with a fresh touch of concern. 'Gone half past nine,' he said. 'I mustn't keep you, and I've got things to do myself.' He took his cup, but did not sit down again. He drank it standing, not hurriedly, but as a matter of business. Its heat did not seem to worry him. Hurst took a sip or two of his and then put his cup down and got to his feet too. He went towards the front door, but Merrow moved towards the kitchen. 'I'll go this way, if you don't mind,' he said.

Hurst said, 'Of course,' and followed him. He understood at once what he meant, because the back door was his private door, and he understood Merrow's wish to be private. Merrow opened the door and went out. Then he stopped and turned.

'You'll take your time, of course,' he said, and Hurst nodded. Then he turned again and went off down the drive to the side road. Hurst stood for a moment looking after him. Then he shut the door and went back into the sitting-room. He finished his cup of tea, as Merrow had, without sitting down, put it back on the tray, put Merrow's cup on the tray with the other things and carried the tray into the kitchen.

He had dressed and breakfasted and gone out into the sunlight at the back of the house when he heard the car stop on the side road at the bottom of the drive. You could not see much of the road from here because of the curve of the hill. He stood still and listened, wondering whether it was anything to do with him. There was nothing else there to stop a car for. On the other hand, if anyone had come to see him in a car, he would expect them to bring it up the drive. It looked a bit inaccessible from the road, but in fact it was easy enough, with plenty of turning space at the top. He went along the path that joined the drive from the back of the cottage and started to walk down. As he came over the shoulder, he saw Christabel walking up the drive towards him. Her car was parked down by the gate. He could not see what it was from here, but it looked small and dark and moderately expensive. It would be her personal car. Christabel looked moderately expensive, too. He was no expert on women's clothes, but there was no mistaking the style. Or perhaps all clothes looked expensive on Christabel, just as some women looked mass-produced whatever you knew they must have spent. He went on down to meet her. She had never been to the cottage before. The curious ease John Merrow had left with him had still not evaporated, and he did not think Christabel had the power to disturb it. He felt interested and a little moved, but the feeling was not unpleasant.

When they came up to each other, she looked more uncertain than he did, and when they spoke, she seemed a little breathless, though that could have been no more than her walk up the steep drive. He said, 'Hullo, Christabel, how nice to see you.'

'Good morning, Mike. Look. I came along because it's rather short notice and you won't have a telephone. We wondered whether you could dine with us this evening.'

'I'd like to very much. What sort of time?'

'Oh – say, half past seven?'

'Fine. I'm afraid I haven't got a black tie here. Does that matter?'

'Good heavens, no. Charles always wears a dog-collar, anyway.'

'Good,' he said. 'Half past seven, neat but not gaudy.'

They stood there on the drive looking at each other till Christabel half turned and said, 'Well —'

Hurst said, 'Won't you come up? I could give you a cup of coffee or something,' and she turned again. She still seemed curiously uncertain of herself.

'Shall I?' she said. 'I've never seen your cottage.'

'I know that, my dear girl. It was not for any want of effort on my part. But that's all a long time ago. So why not come up now?'

She said, 'All right,' and they walked up the drive together. They walked slowly, side by side, not speaking. When they got to the top, she stopped and looked round her. 'What a lovely position,' she said. 'I always thought it looked nice, even from below. Is the spinney yours?'

'Oh yes. I just about own the hill, what there is of it. It's barely a couple of acres, in fact, but it looks more because of its shape.'

'It's lovely.'

'Do you mind using the back door?'

'Of course not.'

He opened it and took her through the kitchen into the sitting-room, and she walked across and stood looking out of the window just as John Merrow had done a couple of hours earlier. She said, 'That's Mrs. Basset's cottage down there?' She spoke without turning round.

'That's it. Would you like coffee?'

She shook her head. She was still looking out of the window. 'No, don't bother, Mike. I mustn't stay. But thank you all the same.'

He came up and stood behind her, but she still did not turn round. He said, 'What's the trouble, Christabel?' He suddenly felt sorry for her, as he had the other morning. It was something in her voice. He did not want to feel sorry for Christabel. It upset his preconceived attitudes, and that made him feel unsafe.

'I don't know.' She turned and faced him. He had heard it said that marriage improved women's looks, but with Christabel that hardly seemed possible. Perhaps it had

39

merely improved her. There was more scope for improvement there. She was still, to his eyes, almost faultlessly beautiful, but the element of danger was no longer present, or if it was, he was no longer conscious of it. You could love this woman, he thought, and not be enslaved by her. Perhaps that was what Charles Richards did. Perhaps it was his doing, this change in her, but he somehow doubted that. If anything had changed in Christabel, it would be she who had changed it. She said, 'I wish you hadn't come back, Mike.'

'I'm sorry,' he said. 'Why, do you know?'

She shrugged. 'Not really. Perhaps because it takes me back, having you here. I don't want to be taken back, Mike.'

'You're sure you want me to come this evening?'

'Oh yes, please. I want you to meet Charles. What about you?'

'I'll come, of course, if you want me to.'

'Yes, but I mean, what about you yourself? Are you any nearer whatever it was you came back for?'

'Not really, no.'

She suddenly moved past him and went towards the door of the kitchen. 'I'm glad of that,' she said. 'Whatever it was, I don't think I'd have liked it.' She went through the kitchen and opened the back door, and he followed her out into the sunlight. 'I'll go now,' she said. 'See you this evening, then.'

'All right.' He stood there and watched her until she disappeared over the shoulder of the drive. Presently he heard the car start. The sound of the engine rose and fell and rose again. It fell and rose several times. Then it rose for the last time and grew fainter until he could no longer hear it. She had backed the car in the gateway and driven back the way she had come, which was not the most direct way to Frantham.

V

He had got his dark trousers and shoes on, and was fitting a
tie under the collar of a decent shirt, when he heard Elizabeth call from downstairs. He looked at his watch, a little
put out because there would be explaining to do, and there
was not too much time left for explanations. He called,
'Half a minute. I'm just coming down.' He finished his tie,
checked his hair, put on his jacket and made sure he had
what he wanted in his various pockets. Then he shut the
door of the bedroom behind him and went downstairs. The
stairs came down into the kitchen, but Elizabeth was not
there. She would have come in by the front door into the
sitting-room, but she had come through into the kitchen to
call up to him. Now she had gone back into the sitting-room
to wait for him, shutting the door between. In the old days
she would probably have come upstairs after him. He
paused and took a breath before he opened the door, just as
he had before he had opened the front door to her the other
evening. She was standing with her back to the windows,
facing him as he came in. She had changed out of her office
dress into something easier. She still looked very nice, but
he was the smart one now. She took this in at once, and her
eyebrows went up.

'Going out?' she said.

He nodded. 'I'm dining at the vicarage.' He gave the
words an ironical touch, because this was the way she
would want it.

'Are you?' she said. 'Good. That sounds all very social

and respectable. You never dined with Mrs. Garstin, did you?'

He shook his head, smiling at her. 'Never once,' he said.

'Well, there you are, then. I told you she was playing it safe. You went and saw her, I take it?'

'I did, yes.' She plainly did not know of Christabel's visit here, and he was not going to tell her.

'Are you in a hurry?'

He looked at his watch, though he already knew what the time was. 'I must go in about five minutes,' he said.

She said, 'Damn. Tell me quickly, then.'

'Tell you what?'

She almost stamped in her impatience. 'Oh, don't be so irritating,' she said. 'About her, of course. About her and you. How did you find her? What did she have to say to you? Apart from asking you to dinner, I mean.'

He said, 'I think I shall go back to calling you Lizz after all.'

She was suddenly very quiet. 'I don't mind what you call me, Mike,' she said. 'But it isn't Lizz asking you. It's me. I know the difference if you don't.'

'I'm sorry. I didn't mean to be provoking. But you are rather rushing me, and it isn't easy. She's changed, Lizz. You said she wouldn't have, but she has.'

'Changed how?'

He thought for a moment. 'I'm no longer afraid of her,' he said.

'That's how you've changed, not Christabel. Or isn't it? No, perhaps you're right. But I'm not sure I like it, anyway. Did you meet the husband?'

'Not yet. I shall this evening, of course. I may know more then, don't you think?'

'Not necessarily. Not about her. But I'll be interested to hear what you make of him, in any case. I've done no more

42

than see him in the street. I'm not one of his flock, exactly. He's liked, I think. I mean, not only the women.'

'I'll tell you all I can, I promise.'

'All right. Go on. You'd better go.'

He said, 'Lizz —,' but she cut him off short.

'No,' she said, 'it's no use, Mike. You go on and keep your date.' She turned and opened the door. 'Enjoy yourself,' she said. 'You still can if you try. It's time you faced up to that.' She went off down the path. He shut the door after her and locked it. Then he went out through the back to get his car out.

He did in fact enjoy himself, despite an initial determination to prove Lizz wrong, or at least to confirm his own assumption that she must be. It was a purely social enjoyment, which seemed irrelevant to his private feelings. Even if this enjoyment had lain mostly in the company of Christabel, he might have been more conscious of the depths beneath, but it did not. It lay almost entirely in the company of Charles Richards. Christabel graced the occasion as it was graced by the good food and wine and the pleasant furnishings of the meal, but the occasion itself was his meeting with Charles. He did not know, or even particularly trouble to ask, whether Christabel was doing this deliberately, or resented it, or was merely unconscious of it. He assumed, without examining the assumption, that he would find this out later when next he met her alone. For the moment it was Charles he was concerned with.

Charles Richards was a big man and completely assured. He wore his faith and his dog-collar as naturally as he wore his health and good looks and even his financial competence, and Hurst had never before met a clergyman who did this. He had met both wary defensiveness and hearty over-compensation, but here there was no need of either. Charles was simply the better man, and his superiority was pleasant and attractive because he himself made no comparisons. It was obvious at once how wrong Mrs. Basset had been to find anything amusing in his marriage with Christabel. To be amused at it was to imply that in some respect he did not know what he was doing, but in this as in most other matters Charles Richards would know what he was doing perfectly well and have no doubts about it. It was also apparent why Christabel herself had been so insistent that the two should meet. Once you had met the husband, you understood how safe she was and where her safety lay. It was important to her that you should understand this, because the understanding itself reinforced her own sense of safety. Feeling as he now did about Christabel, he was glad of this, directly for her sake, but mainly, though less directly, for his own. Meanwhile, he surrendered himself to his enjoyment of the occasion. It would be time enough to consider its implications when he got home.

The meal was managed smoothly, with the three of them looking after themselves, and unseen hands ministering on the far side of the service hatch. It was only when it was over that Christabel went off to see to the coffee and the men were left alone. Charles Richards did not go in for the ceremonial handling of port, but he poured Hurst out another glass of wine, which in any case he preferred. Then he leant back in his chair and said, 'I think Christabel's a bit worried about you. Did you know?'

Hurst hesitated. There was no question of prevarication, because you did not prevaricate with this man. He hesitated because he wanted to get the answer right, and he was not sure what the right answer was. He said, 'Worried about me?', stressing the 'about' slightly, and Richards took him up on it.

'You mean, as opposed to worried by you? I think so. I can't be altogether sure. I suppose it could be a little of both.' He stopped there. He had modified the question slightly, but Hurst still had to answer it.

He said, 'I think it is possible that she may be worried about me. I admit it's an idea which takes some getting used to. If she is to any extent worried by me, I think it would be only a sort of by-product of the other worry. Does that answer your question?'

'To some extent. I have certainly formed the impression that you are a man with troubles of your own. If so, they are no business of mine, and I am not concerned with them, as I am, of course, with Christabel's. I mean,' he added, 'as a mere man I am not. As a priest I am concerned with anyone's troubles, but I am not speaking to you as a priest. Why do you say that the idea takes some getting used to?'

Hurst smiled slightly, because he felt a smile was called for, but he spoke quite seriously. 'Because when I knew her before, I didn't think she worried very much about anyone, certainly not about me.'

Richards nodded. 'I assume you were in a greater or less degree in love with her, because I assume that, as things then were, almost any unattached man must have been. I don't think you any longer are – I mean, even apart from the changed circumstances. To be in love with a woman who does not love you is necessarily to put yourself to some extent at her mercy. Don't you think that when this happens, you may be inclined to attribute to her a lack of concern which may not be altogether just? Any love for another person is to some extent selfish, and if the love is one-sided, the element of selfishness is apt to increase rather than otherwise.'

'Yes, all right, I accept that. At any rate, I agree that the fact that I am no longer in love with her, which of course is true, may work both ways. It may enable me to recognise in Christabel a concern that I couldn't see before. I think it may also allow her in fact to feel a concern she did not feel before. There is the other side of the medal, you know. To have someone in love with you when you are not in love with them can breed a sort of defensive mercilessness, don't you think? It may even have its healthy side – being cruel only to be kind, that sort of thing.'

Richards said at once, 'That's perfectly true. I of all people shouldn't forget that. To have women fall in love with him, or think they are in love with him, is, as you know, an occupational hazard for the parish priest, just as it is for the doctor, and even, I am told, for the driving instructor. It is for the priest it poses the worst problems, because sympathy is an essential part of his stock in trade. And of course you are perfectly right. A kind of mercilessness can be called for. The priest who turns such love to account, even for the best of purposes, isn't really doing his job.' He finished his wine, and Hurst, as though in obedience to a signal, finished his. 'As to your own troubles,' Richards said, 'I don't know how much Christabel knows about them. I haven't, obviously, discussed it with her.'

He got up. Hurst got up too, and said, 'As far as I know, nothing at all.'

Richards nodded. 'Then I ask to know nothing, either,' he said. 'If you choose to come to me as to a priest, I am at your disposal, and will do the best I can. In the confessional, simply as such, I do not believe. There will be coffee in the other room. Shall we go?'

Christabel sat with the coffee tray in front of her. She looked at them as a woman looks at two men when she has private strings to each of them and is wondering, now that they have been alone together, whether they have got them crossed. There was no apprehension in the look, only a sort of re-appraisal. They both, in their different ways, smiled at her, and she smiled back, comprehensively, and turned her eyes down to the coffee things.

The catwalk of social enjoyment, on which he had picked his way contentedly the whole evening, suddenly collapsed under him, and Hurst found himself engulfed in the familiar depths of irresolution and despair. There was bitterness in it too, a sense of almost incredulous indignation, to see this beautiful woman sitting so warm and secure behind her porcelain and silverware, when she had brought him to this pass. If he had still been in love with her, the thing would at least have been intelligible, and to that extent more tolerable. But he no longer was. There was nothing left at all except the facts, and the facts he could not cope with. He took his cup with a hand that was, momentarily, not altogether steady, and when he sat down with it, he saw that Richards was watching him. Then his practised hold on himself re-asserted itself, and he smiled on the company. He said, 'It is usually the woman's line to say how much she has enjoyed a meal she hasn't had to cook herself. All the same, the pleasure is a real one. I don't mean only the food, of course. The whole way the thing is done. No one who lives alone ever really lives the civilised life. Unless, I suppose, he is prepared to devote nearly all his attention to being civilised, and most of us aren't.'

Richards said, 'Taking civilisation in the rather limited sense you have in mind, it would surely be a wrong choice if he did.'

'Oh, that's true, of course. There are too many other things to do. But laziness plays a good part in it. The mere effort is too much.'

Christabel said, 'There's a middle course, surely. Pigging it would be worse than overdoing it. I'm sure you don't pig it.'

He laughed. He heard his laugh in a detached sort of way, and was pleased with it. 'I hope not, indeed,' he said.

'All the same, it doesn't need an exclusive diet of husks to make one appreciate the occasional fatted calf.'

Richards said, 'Surely it wasn't only the food that the prodigal son appreciated, or even the robes and the ring. The love was the thing.'

For a moment Hurst held his breath, and the two men looked at each other. Then Hurst nodded. 'Oh yes,' he said, 'that I don't doubt.' A sort of lunatic hope touched him, as it had when he had been speaking to John Merrow. Now as then, he could not put an intelligible shape on it, and it was too impalpable to last. Something to do with love, though, not his, other people's. It was nothing to do with his feelings at all. That was why he could not get hold of it. Christabel was watching the pair of them again, and he wondered suddenly if it might be she who was for the moment the outsider, not himself at all. But the exclusion could not last, because the thing itself was too intangible to exclude anybody for long.

She said, 'I suppose in any case the cottage here is not your real home. At least, it must be very difficult to have two real homes, and you've been away from here for a long time.'

He thought of the dark flat, and of how little had happened to him there physically and how much in his mind. It was not really particularly dark, but he thought of it as dark because of what had happened there. He knew in any case that, once he had left it, he could not go back there, or not to live. That was one of the things that frightened him. He did not know what could happen to him here, but he had nowhere else to go back to. He said, 'It's difficult to say. I certainly felt this was my home once. Now I'm not sure.' He could prevaricate with Christabel. Richards was watching him, but did not intervene.

She said, 'I wondered if you would want to keep the cottage on, or whether perhaps you had come back with the idea of getting rid of it.'

John Merrow had wondered this, too. People would, of course, though it had not occurred to him that they would. Only John Merrow had had his own solution to the problem. The problem was his, and Merrow had offered him a solution to it. That was the way he saw it, and he believed Merrow saw it like that too. Of course Merrow wanted the cottage for himself, but his interest in it was more disinterested than Christabel's. He said, 'I hadn't really thought about it. I suppose I might.'

Richards said, 'I shouldn't be in too much of a hurry. Take your time.' That was exactly what Merrow had said, and he did not think it was what Christabel wanted. He wondered if Richards understood this. He thought perhaps he did, but had said it all the same. Once more he saw Christabel momentarily as the third party, and he was sure that this time she felt it. He assumed, again, that he would see her some time alone, and he wondered how, when he did, she would deal with it.

He said, 'Oh yes, I must think about it, of course.' He said it lightly, because he did not want the thing to be taken any further between the three of them. 'The book's the immediate problem,' he said. 'I have got to get started again with that.' This was true in a sense, and at least it made something to talk about. Richards had read one of his books, which Christabel had not, but here the division of interest was an acceptable one.

They talked about books until he thought it would be reasonable for him to go. They both came to the door to see him off, and he had the curious feeling that for all of them there was safety in numbers. The sky was overcast again and the night dark. For the moment the fair weather was over. He drove slowly through the lanes, coming at the cot-

tage by the side road, as Christabel had done earlier in the
day. All the same, he could not go up the drive without the
lights, and if anyone was watching, they would know he was
back, even if he did not put the lights on in the sitting-
room. Not that anyone would come, even if they knew he
was there. It was too late for that.

VI

He was awakened, in physical terms, by the noise of the wind round the house and the threshing of the trees outside his window. When he came fully to his senses, he saw there was a grey early daylight outside, and for a moment he found this difficult to understand, like an exhausted man who has slept the clock round and does not know what time it is. He tried to remember what he had done during the night, but could remember nothing. It was only gradually, as if he was afraid to let himself jump to conclusions, that he faced the fact that he had slept all night. He could not have said when he had last done this, but it must have been a long time ago. When he did accept the fact, he shut his eyes again and turned over in bed, shielding his face from the light. His body seemed twice its normal weight, like a dead body when you tried to carry it. Something had happened to his mind, too. It must have been a dream, but he could not remember it, because it had not awakened him, as most of his dreams did. He wanted to remember it as much as he wanted to forget most of his other dreams, but all he had left was the effect it had on his mind. He thought if he could get to sleep again, he might manage to hold on to this, perhaps even to slip back into the dream that had produced it. He knew it would not stand up to the pressures of his waking mind. He tried to surrender himself to the weight of his body and the lightness of his mind, but the effort was a conscious one, and its effect was self-defeating. Gradually but inexorably his body began to tense and lift itself from the bed and his mind grew heavy with its accustomed burden. He was awake, after all, and could do nothing about it. Something had happened to him, but he could not say what it was, except for the unarguable physical fact that he had slept through from night to morning. After a bit he got up and put on his dressing-gown and slippers and went downstairs. His body, which had seemed so heavy in the bed, now moved with an unaccustomed speed and lightness, so that even the simplest actions seemed easier than usual, and the grey chill of the morning did not worry him.

Even when he was up and dressed, he was obsessed with the idea that there was a way out of his predicament which he had not previously thought of. He did not know what it was, or even in what direction to look for it between the different courses which he had followed, one after the other, over and over again in his imagination and found in their different ways intolerable in practice. Only the conviction remained that the way was there, and that he had had it in his sleep but lost it again. The conviction still gave him what seemed an almost physical relief and comfort, but did not in itself suggest a course of action. He occupied himself with chores about the house, balancing himself instinctively on the mental level they demanded and allowed him to maintain. He even got out the case containing his working papers, which he had brought with him as a matter of course, but had not opened since his arrival. Now he opened it and spread the papers out on his working table, but the fear of what might happen if he tried to concentrate his mind on them held him back. Instead he left them there, all ready for him to start work when the moment came, and put on his raincoat and cap and went out of the house. He thought of going for a walk, but did not trust this either. Instead he got the car out and drove into Frantham to shop.

Most of the people in the shops had known him in the old days, but even then few of them could have put a name to him. He never ran up bills, and was not in himself the sort of person to make more than a purely personal impression on any community. Even the people who had known him would mostly have forgotten him by now, and in any case there were new faces everywhere. Nowadays a place like Frantham turned over a surprisingly large part of its working population in five years. He shopped pleasantly but anonymously. He met no one from the Vicarage in the streets, and if Lizz saw him from behind the screened window of the solicitors', she had no way of telling him she had or he of knowing. It was only at the end, when he had put all his things in the car and was on his way home, that the man at the garage challenged him. He took the money for the petrol, and Hurst followed him back to his office to collect his change. Like many such, it was rather cluttered and dark, and smelt faintly of oil. Even the girl on the calendar looked slightly shop-soiled, as if she had been turned over by hastily wiped hands. The man paused over his till, looking at him with a sort of hesitant sharpness. He said, 'Aren't you the gentleman that used to live out Furzehill way? Mr. Hurst, isn't it?'

Hurst said, 'That's quite right. I still do, in fact, only I've been away for a bit.'

'Ah,' the man said, 'that's it. Thought I knew you.' He sorted out the change and passed it over, looking at Hurst and sucking his teeth. Then he said, 'Do you know anything about a chap called Jack Basset?'

Hurst put the change in his pocket without looking at it. 'Not now,' he said. 'I used to know him. He's not there now.'

'I know that. You haven't any idea where he'd be?'

Hurst shook his head. 'Afraid not,' he said.

They looked at each other and the man dropped his eyes and shut the drawer of the till. 'Hope you don't mind my asking,' he said. 'The fact is, he owed us quite a bit, and we've never seen our money. I wouldn't mind a word with young Jack. But nobody seems to know where he's gone to, or if they do, they aren't saying.'

Hurst said, 'Sorry I can't help you.'

The man smiled at him, friendly again, but still a little foxy. 'Well,' he said, 'people go off owing for petrol and that. One's used to that. But Jack bought a car from us, a used car of course. We never had no proper agreement, but he was paying all right by the month. Then he just went. And he didn't take the car with him. He sold it in Astbury before he left and took the cash. We come to know because there was some question about the registration, but we couldn't do nothing. It was his car, legally. Only he hadn't half paid us for it. Well, I don't know what you think, but I call that cheating. We should have known him better, I suppose. I've heard more about him since, but people don't talk till a chap's gone. Then it all comes out. We aren't the only ones suffered. But no one knows where he's gone to, and I don't suppose we ever will. Only I thought it was worth asking, seeing that you live close, but aren't one of the family. We've tried them, of course.'

Hurst said, 'They don't know where he is, either. You can take that for a fact. You'll do no good bothering them.' He spoke a little fiercely, and the man looked at him.

'No one's bothering anyone,' he said. 'Only if you lose track of a debtor, you ask where you can. That's natural.'

'Of course I understand that.' Hurst was almost apologetic. 'Only as I say, his mother and sister don't hear from him. From what they said, I don't think he's missed much, in fact.'

The man was all mollification, too, now. 'No, well,' he said, 'they're decent people, I know that. He was a right bastard, if you ask me. One for the women, though. They loved him. I don't know how well you know him.'

'Not well. He didn't talk much, as far as I can remember. But I didn't like him, no.'

'He talked too much for us,' the man said. 'Big mouth, he had, when he come here. Still, he paid regular while he did pay. We couldn't know he was going to pull that on us.'

Hurst was back in his car by now. He said again, 'Well, sorry I can't be of more help,' and they nodded to each other as he drove off. One for the women, he thought. They loved him. What he remembered above all about Jack Basset was his vulgarity. It had been a mainly physical quality because his mind had been secretive rather than blatant. But the physical quality was unmistakable. He remembered the strong, stocky body with a faintly exaggerated vigour of movement, especially about the shoulders, as if the body swaggered of itself and the mind was too insensitive to control its swagger. The skin was fresh-coloured but rather greasy, the hair curled close to the head, the eyes had the same unconscious insolence as the body. Every man knew this type of man and the effect it had on the darker side of women. That was the unforgivable thing about it. Otherwise it was negligible. Every man treasured the darker side of women and wanted to keep it to himself, when it was the one thing he could not monopolise. The lighter side was his to keep if he wanted it and earned it, which half the time he did not. But it was the darker side that enslaved him, and the darker side was there for the Jack Bassets of the world as well as for himself, and the women accepted this, and could not see, until the harm was done, what all the fuss was about. That was the ultimate, irreconcilable difference, the effortless dichotomy of the woman and the tortured unity of the man. The wonder was that anything ever went right between them. But then how often did it, in the long run? And yet where else, God help all men, was peace to be found?

He did not want to go back to the cottage now, but he had all the things in the car and must take them home and unpack them and put them away, because that was what he always did. For him, as for most people who live alone, an ordered routine provided the essential guide-lines of sanity. But the intimation of hope he had woken to had evaporated irretrievably. The cottage was as dark to his mind as it would be, under this grey sky, to his eyes when he got there. All the same, he drove on, because when all was said and done, he had nowhere else to go.

He did not go near his work table all day, though he saw it in passing. He got himself meals and ate them and cleared away and washed up, and in between he went for a long walk in the fields. It never rained, but the clouds did not move or break. Dusk came early, but even before it was fully dusk outside he had drawn the curtains and turned the lights on. Then at last he sat down at his work table and pulled the essential bundle of papers to him, but before he had opened the cover the finger-tips drummed on the door, and he got up and opened it and let Lizz in. She said, 'Why do I always have to come to you?'

There was no coquetry in it. She seemed to be asking herself the question as much as him. He said, 'I'm always here and I'm alone. I never know whether you're at home or not, and in any case you wouldn't be alone. If I came to you, where should we go, except back here?'

She nodded. 'I suppose that's it. Were you working?'

'No.' He took his failure to work so much for granted that it did not occur to him to explain it.

She said, 'Can't you work, Mike? You'd be happier if you could.'

'I don't know. I think it's the other way round.'

'You mean, if you were happier, you could work? I think

that's an excuse.'

'All right, I know it's an excuse. I still can't work.'

'Anyway, did you enjoy the party?'

'Yes, very much. Most of the time, anyway. I enjoyed meeting him.'

'Tell me,' she said. She still sat opposite him, with most of the width of the room between them. The obvious thing was for him to go across to her and take hold of her. He thought it was as obvious to her as it was to him, but that was the main reason why he could not let himself do it. He would still have to tell her about the party, and taking her in his arms would only complicate things.

He said, 'He's a good man, Lizz.'

'Too good for her?'

'I'm not sure about that. I can't make up my mind about her. Too good for me, anyhow.'

'That's his job,' she said. She was so matter-of-fact about it, she surprised him.

He said, 'I know it's his job. The point is, he does it. So few of them do.'

She nodded. 'Where does she come into it, then?' she said.

'That's what I can't make out, of course. I feel them very much as husband and wife. I wouldn't say as a rule I'm in favour of celibacy for the clergy, but I don't really see how it's managed. I mean in a case like this. So often the vicar's wife is more vicar than the vicar, and of course that works in a way, but he's much better than that. I suppose he's big enough for the two. At any rate, she doesn't get in the way at all.'

'You mean, between you and him? That's good. It's surprising though, I must say.'

'It surprised me,' he said. 'I thought at first it was her doing. But I don't think it was.'

'Doesn't she mind, then?'

He hesitated and she sat there, quite motionless, never taking her eyes off him, just waiting for him to speak. It was what she had used to do in the old days, when he had been the oracle, but the effect now was very different. All the same, his hesitation was real. 'I don't know,' he said. He looked up and met that unwavering stare. 'Don't you see, Lizz? That's what I can't make out.'

She said, 'Does it matter?' She was still looking at him.

'No, I don't think it does, really. Except in some way in relation to him.'

She dropped her eyes then. Her hands were folded in her lap, and she sat there looking down at them. They did not move at all. She said, 'Never mind, I expect she'll tell you, anyway.'

He knew he had made the same assumption himself, but he also knew there was nothing to justify it. He said, 'I don't see why she should,' but her head jerked up angrily.

'I can think of several good reasons why she shouldn't,' she said. 'But I think she will, all the same.'

He suddenly found her anger unbearable, because the quite simple reassurance she needed was the one he could not give and therefore must not even offer. He said, 'Lizz, for heaven's sake, Christabel can do nothing to me now. Or to you. Whatever is done is done. It's up to me now. It doesn't matter what she does. She's no longer involved. You're wasting your anger on her. Can't you see that?'

It was she, after all, who got up. She got up and came across to him and sat herself on the arm of his chair, looking down into his upturned face. There was only the slightest contact, but he could feel the warmth of her and smell, only very faintly even at this close range, whatever it was she smelt of. She was enormously desirable. But she smiled suddenly, as if she was mocking, not him, but the futility of his distress. She spoke very calmly and quietly. She said, 'May I make a suggestion?'

His mouth was dry. He simply nodded, still looking up at her.

'Leave this damned place,' she said, 'and get right away. And take me with you. I can earn my keep wherever we are, and I reckon I can get you working again, if you give me the chance. But the great thing is to get away and not come back. You needn't marry me if you don't want to.'

For a moment he was unmanned by sheer longing to take her hand and go the way she pointed, but he knew it was not really a new way. It was only one of the old ways he had explored often enough in his mind and always finished by rejecting. It led only to disaster, and to take Lizz with him could make it worse, not better. He looked down then, because he could not bear to see her smile so close above him.

She watched his face change, and when it turned away from her, she got up. She got up quite slowly and went back to her place on the other side of the room and sat there, not looking at him. He still said nothing. She said, 'Don't say anything now, Mike, please. Don't say anything at all. I've said what I wanted to say, and that stands. It's there if you want it. Think about it. Or rather, you don't have to think about it, only just know it's there.'

He lifted his head then and for a moment they looked at each other. He said, 'All right, Lizz.' He spoke almost in a whisper, and she nodded and got up and went out of the front door, shutting it quietly behind her.

VII

He had drawn the curtains on the last of the daylight. When he turned the sitting-room lights out, there was still light outside, and he had an odd moment of temporal disorientation, as if the sun had stopped moving or he had at some point got ahead of the day. He went to the window and flicked one curtain aside. It was moonlight, of course. He had lost track of the moon because of the cloudy nights, but now the cloud had broken again, and there it was, nearly a half-moon and quite high in the sky. There was a breeze, too, not enough to hear through the glass, but enough to be visible in moving cloud shadows and a faint shimmer of reflecting surfaces. He got his coat and went out of the front door. He always used the front door at night, just as he always used the back door during the day. He was a great one for evening things up.

He went down the path to the road. There were lights on all over Mrs. Basset's cottage, but all the windows were curtained, and he could see nobody. On the road he turned left, walking on the soft verge at first, and then on the tarmac when he had got well away from the cottage. He walked steadily, but he was in no hurry. What he was making for would wait for him. It was going there that counted. Even when the cloud was over the moon there was plenty of light to walk by, and when it was not, you could see quite long distances, though nothing very clearly. He saw the white gates long before he came to them, but under the trees along the drive it was very dark. All the same, he found his way without difficulty. He had known many such nights, and these were grown trees. They had not changed much in five years.

There was no one on the road in either direction, and when he came to the gates, he just turned and walked straight in. He walked a little way up the drive and then went through the trees to the edge of the grass. The front of the house was blank and white in the moonlight. There were lights behind the curtains in the ground-floor windows, but they looked fainter than they were because of the moonlight outside. He wondered about the Barneses. He knew nothing about them except that they were quiet. He wondered what they would do if he went up and rang the front-door bell and explained why he was interested in their house. It would be nice to tell somebody who was involved like this, but who was neutral, and perhaps they were bored with their quietness and would be glad of a little excitement. He did not for a moment suppose that he would do anything of the sort, and did not even wish to. His mind found these diversions for itself, which were near enough to its problem, but ran parallel with it instead of moving to the same point.

A cloud came over the moon. It must be a black one, because the front of the house almost disappeared, and the windows glowed suddenly out of the darkness with the stealthy, selfconscious effect of stage lighting. He stood in the edge of the trees, waiting. Presently he would walk across the grass to the far end of the house, because that was the only thing he could do. He could not expect anyone to come walking across to him, not even when it was as dark as this and he would not see them until they were quite close to him. They ought to come across in the moonlight, but it was easier to imagine like this, when he could not see that there was no one there. He could not even hear that there was no one walking on the grass, because the trees kept up a faint continuous rustle in the breeze, and feet on the grass do not make much noise.

Then the cloud passed, and the light came up again, by perceptible stages, but quite suddenly. There was somebody coming across the grass towards him. Already they were half-way across. It was not the person he had been imagining, but someone taller. They walked a little stealthily, but quite fast. He could see who it was now. He went forward a little out of the trees, so that she could see him too. He said, 'Hullo, Christabel.'

Just for a moment she stopped, and then she almost ran forward to meet him. She took him by the arms and he stood there, quite passive, looking at her. 'Mike,' she said. 'Oh Mike, you frightened me.'

He said, 'Ghosts shouldn't frighten each other, even if they're on different haunts. Do you know the Barneses?'

'No. Well, yes, I've met them, of course. I don't know them. They don't know I'm here.'

He laughed, but quietly, because they were talking very quietly. He was conscious of some enormous pent-up emotion, but could not quite tell what it was. He said, 'My dear, I can see that. What are you doing here, then?'

Their faces were very close in the moonlight. She did not turn her head, but her eyes went sideways away from his. 'I come here sometimes,' she said. 'When Charles is away. I don't know – just to see the place.'

He nodded. 'How did you get here?' he said. 'I didn't see your car.'

'It's down the road. Not far.'

'Let's go there, then. Come on.' She had taken her hands off his arms, and now he took her, but gently, by one arm and led her out through the trees and down the drive to the gate. The moon had gone in again, but the road was clear enough. He turned left, because he assumed the car would be that way, and she went with him. He had dropped her arm now, and they walked steadily side by side, saying nothing. He wondered what they would do if a car came along, but none did.

Presently she said, 'In there,' and pointed. A small lane led off between high hedges, not much more than a field track. He followed her, and found the dark, sleek car standing between the hedges. It had no lights on and showed up only where the luminescence from the sky caught the body work. It looked full of stealthy passion in the back seat, but Christabel had come here only to walk by herself in the garden of a house she had once owned. As things were these days, she was running a fearful risk even to leave it there like that where it might be recognised, but she had presumably taken this into account. He wondered what she would do now they were both here, but she showed no hesitation at all. She walked straight up to the car, unlocked it and got into the driving seat. Then she leant across and opened the near-side door. 'Get in,' she said.

Just for a moment he hesitated. He still did not know where he was with her at all, or even with himself. Then he got in and shut the door. It was pitch dark. When the moon came out again there would be a glimmer of light from the narrow line of the sky between the hedges ahead of them, but now there was none. He could smell something very faint and expensive, but the car might smell like that whether she was in it or not. She sat absolutely motionless, but if he held his breath, he could just hear her breathing. She breathed lightly and rather fast, as if her mouth was a little open. He said, 'Christabel, this is crazy.' He spoke very quietly, although there was no one to hear. 'If anyone sees the car here, you know what they'll think. It's not only you I'm thinking of. It isn't fair on Charles.'

She said, 'No one will. No one ever comes here at night.'

Her voice was curiously flat and expressionless, as if what she said was an automatic response to an outside stimulus and not what her mind was really working on. He wanted badly to say something, but still did not know what it was he wanted to say. She said, 'Why did you say we were on different haunts? Just now, I mean.' She still kept her voice low, but now it was vibrant with an urgency that seemed almost desperation.

He did not like this. He had said what he had said almost to himself, because at that moment all that had been needed was for him to say something. He had not expected to be taken up and cross-examined on it. 'I'm not sure what I meant,' he said. 'But I mean – you lived in the house. You were brought up there mostly, weren't you? It was yours after your mother's death. Of course it would mean something to you it wouldn't mean to me.'

The moon came out from behind its cloud, and in the faint reflected light he could just see her face as she swung round suddenly in the seat to face him. She stared into his face, with her eyes wide open and her mouth, as he had thought, very slightly open too. He thought he could feel her breath on his face. She said, 'That's right. It was my home. Of course I remember things. But you only came there to see me.'

He had nothing to say to this, and for a moment they stared at each other in silence, their faces almost touching. When she spoke again, her voice was no more than a throaty whisper. 'It's the same haunt,' she said. 'Mike, I tell you, it's the same haunt. Don't you see?'

The moon went in again, and in the sudden dense darkness her mouth closed over his. The lips were parted and moist, and he felt her hands run ferreting over him, digging into his arms and body with strong, febrile fingers. For a moment he was passive under her attack. There was no desire in him at all, and he sat there flaccid and impotent while her body worked on his. Then a sort of horrified pity welled up in him, and he put out his strength and pushed her away. She said, 'No, Mike. Mike —,' struggling to keep her face to his. Revulsion turned suddenly to anger, and he pulled one hand free and smacked her sharply on the side of her face.

For a moment she froze as he held her. Then her body keeled away from him sideways, so that he could no longer see her in the darkness, but he heard her crying as though her heart would break. He put out a hand and took a gentle hold on her arm, and one of her hands came up and closed over his. He said, 'I'm sorry, Christabel, I'm sorry,' but she said nothing, only went on crying quietly in her seat beside him.

After a little the sobbing died away, and she said, 'Oh God,' in a small strangled voice. He said nothing, and a moment later she spoke again. Her voice was clearer now. 'Why did you come back?' she said. 'I told you I wished you hadn't. What did you come here for if it wasn't that?'

He said, 'Christabel, you've got to understand. You've got to think. It's not so long ago. Don't you remember what you did to me?'

'What did I do to you?' She spoke in a quiet deadly voice, and then, when he hesitated, she raised her voice and almost shouted at him. 'Go on, tell me what I did to you.'

He was quite determined now. He could see his way ahead. He said, 'All right, I'll tell you what you did. I was in love with you. You knew that. I was in love with you from the first time I saw you, and you knew it and did nothing to stop it. And then all of a sudden you gave yourself to me, that night in your room. You gave yourself to me in a way no woman's ever given herself to me, before or since, and I thought we'd be lovers for ever, and I was in heaven. But I was wrong, in fact. It wasn't the beginning of anything, it was the end of everything. You had nothing more to give. I suppose you'd had what you wanted. I couldn't believe it at first. When I did, I thought I'd go out of my mind. I think I did a little. That's what you did to me. If you'd left me alone, I'd have got over it. Anyone does, in time, if there's no chance and nothing much happens. Or if you'd gone on with what you started – I don't know in the long run, but it would have been heaven at the time. But you did neither the one nor the other, and that was deadly. I can't tell you how deadly. I don't know about women. All I know is that when that's happened to a man, he's lost. I was lost, and you let it happen. That was when I went away. It burns itself out, of course, one way or another, in time. That's just self-preservation. Then it's gone for ever. It was gone for ever before I came back here, or I shouldn't have come.'

It was still pitch dark in the car. He could not see her, and she did not move or speak. After a bit he said, 'Come on, Christabel. It's time you went home. I'm sorry I hit you, but you'll be glad tomorrow. There's still Charles.'

She said, 'It's nothing to do with Charles. Charles is a separate thing altogether. Nothing you and I could do could touch Charles.' She spoke in a curiously calm, matter-of-fact way, as if she was stating what ought to be obvious to both of them. 'It's just me. Another part of me. It's always been there.'

His moment of gentleness was past. He was angry again now. He said, 'Then keep it away from me. I've had it once, and I don't want it again. Now I'll get out and see you out on to the road. Then you go off home. I expect we'll see each other again, but so far as I'm concerned, this hasn't happened.'

She said, 'All right,' and he got out into the lesser darkness outside and shut the door of the car behind him. He walked out of the lane on to the tarmac, and as he got there, the moon came out, and he saw that the last of the cloud had gone and the whole sky was clear. The country lay remote and ivory-coloured, with not even the cloud shadows to disturb it. In the near hedges the occasional leaf flickered with reflected light, and at one point ahead of him the tarmac shone like silver where the moon caught it. He looked back into the lane, and a moment later he heard the engine start and the car lights went on. The red glow turned to white as the gears were put into reverse, and at once the car began to move. It backed out steadily on to the road. There was no hesitation and the engine note never wavered. It was all very competent and practised. He stood clear as the car came on to the tarmac. He could just see a figure at the wheel, but it did not look at him or make any sort of signal. It might have been anybody. The car came round in a smooth curve and lost way and then went smoothly forward, so that he could not have said at what precise moment it was stationary. Only the white reversing lights went out, and the red lights glared and then receded and he was left standing alone in the moonlight.

He began walking at once. He was still angry, and he did not want to hesitate any more than the car had done. Even though there was no one to see him, he did not want to be left standing there. He did not walk fast, because he had no distance to go and no wish to be home, but the important thing was to be moving. The anger died out of him as he moved, and his mind filled slowly with an enormous, useless regret. It was not regret for the experience he had rejected, which he still did not want. It was more a regret for the fact that he no longer wanted it, for the whole vicious, self-destructive process that even at this level had taken the purpose and desire out of him and lost him the capacity for positive action. Later on it was his anger he regretted. He had no right to be angry at something which not so long ago he would have given twenty years of his life for, and just because he no longer wanted it. He had no right to be angry with Christabel at all, and to slap her face, even in a moment of near-panic, had been indefensible. You could never, in the long run, blame anyone else for anything you did, whatever it looked like at the time. Christabel had been angry with him at the end, and by God, she had had reason to be.

For perhaps the first time he felt a simple and sympathetic affection for her, which by-passed the obtrusive physical qualities and fixed on the person for whom, no less than for the rest of the world, they were a distortion and a danger. She had said Charles was away, and now she would be getting back, as he was, to fading anger, and regret, and a room with no one else in it and the moonlight white outside. The urge to make it up to her was so strong that if she had had further to travel, and he himself had been in his car, he would have gone after her. But it was useless now. She would have put her car away and be inside the vicarage before he had even got his out of the garage, and there must be no more haunting of houses tonight. Least of all of Frantham vicarage. Perhaps after all she was still angry, and her anger left no room for regret. He hoped that was so. He went straight up the path in the moonlight. He did not remember, afterwards, whether there had still been lights on in Mrs. Basset's cottage or not. The moonlight was so bright that he would hardly have noticed them if there were.

VIII

He was sorry for too many people now, and yet when he had come here, he had been sorry only for Mrs. Basset, and that only in a nagging, uncertain sort of way. Now he did not think he was sorry for Mrs. Basset at all, but he was sorry for Lizz because of what seemed to be happening to her, and he was sorry for Christabel because of what had happened between them, and he was sorry for Charles Richards because of Christabel. He was even sorry for John Merrow, because he could not offer him the escape he wanted from a predicament that obviously worried him. It was perhaps not a very serious predicament, but it was understandable. A man like Merrow would not want to be cast indefinitely in the role of Roger the lodger. He was not sorry for himself, because, living the life he did, he could never manage to be sorry for himself over anything except purely fortuitous disasters, like toothache or a flat tyre. Everything else that happened to him was likely to be his own doing, and that precluded self-pity. If he indulged himself in any way it was only in the belief that he could not go on as he was, and this was not a conscious self-indulgence. At any rate it had brought him back, only now he was here he seemed less than ever able to see any alternative. Some intimation had touched him for a moment after his evening at the vicarage, but he had not been able to tie it down, and now it was lost completely. He had not had a proper night's sleep since that night, and in the kind of sleep he got intimations did not come.

It was at the far end of a long and arid walk that he came

out into a tiny village he did not know with a telephone call-box at the corner. He went straight in, looked up the number and dialled the Frantham vicarage. He did not know how long Charles Richards had been away, but he thought he would be back by now. If he was not, he need not speak to anyone else, but the voice that answered was Charles's. He said who he was, and Charles said, 'Oh, hullo, yes. I have been rather expecting you to get in touch with me.'

Hurst found his mouth dry, but he had to know. He said, 'Since when?'

'Well, since the evening you dined with us. I formed the impression that there was something you might decide you would like to talk about. But perhaps I was wrong.'

'No,' said Hurst, 'you were right. There is.'

'You are coming to me as a priest?'

'Yes, I suppose so. But then I am hardly a Christian. More, perhaps, as one in authority.'

'I see. I expect it's the same thing. Well, look here, will you come to the church? We can talk quite privately in the vestry. I shan't put you in a confessional box. We don't have them. But I like to make a distinction between a meeting of this sort and a business meeting, even parochial business. I don't like business in the church and I don't like this sort of meeting at the vicarage. Will you do that?'

'Of course.'

'Good. Well —' He paused a moment, and Hurst heard the faint rustle of papers. 'Can you come at five tomorrow? I've got to go out at six, but we can have an hour.'

'Yes. Thank you. I'll be there.'

'Good. And look here. I cannot very effectively speak with authority if you do not recognise the authority that has been given me. But I'll do what I can to help. You may recognise more than you think. Till tomorrow, then.'

They said good-bye and rang off, and Hurst turned to

70

the long walk home. He was a little breathless, but pleased with what he had done. Even to hear Charles Richards's voice was an assurance. Above all, he had committed himself to a specific course of action at five the next evening. He did not know at all what might come of it, or even see what could, but for the moment he need not look beyond it, and that gave him peace of a sort for twenty-four hours.

He went through the routine motions of living with a curious numb concentration, so that they occupied completely what was left of his mind, like a sick man learning to walk again and conscious of nothing beyond the need to get his legs working. There were things in his day, things he did while making his bed or particular moments in the process of washing up, which from some forgotten association, and now from sheer emotional habit, filled him with an almost terrifying despair every time he did them. He never remembered them until he came to them, so that the misery on each occasion took him by surprise, and he could not take steps to avoid it, even if the actions themselves had been avoidable. Now he negotiated these pitfalls without mishap, unconscious of each particular failure of the trigger mechanism, but conscious of a general and continuous freedom from the immediate threat of pain. It was only as the time came near for his meeting that apprehension awoke again, but it was not the meeting he feared so much as what might lie beyond it.

The church was dark and empty when he went into it. He latched the heavy wooden door behind him as quietly as he could, and the silence and the smell of old stone shut him in. For a moment he stood there, utterly unable to think why he had come or what he had to do. Then a door in the western end of the church opened, and Charles Richards came out from behind a panelled screen. He was not wearing canonicals and looked reassuringly human and alive. He said, 'Good. Come on in,' and Hurst went over to him, tip-toeing over the flagged floor of the nave.

A light burned in the vestry and an electric heater took the chill out of the air. On two sides of it the stone walls ran up into what must be the base of the tower. On the other two a high wooden screen partitioned it effectively from the main body of the church. A rather worn carpet covered most of the flagstones. There was a cupboard, a writing table, a few chairs and a curtained recess which probably held the vicar's vestments. Faintly incongruous but somehow reassuring, the door of a heavy safe showed in one wall. That would be the church plate. The vestry was a small human enclave in the numinous emptiness, and Charles Richards looked thoroughly at home in it. He sat down in the chair at the table and pointed Hurst to another beside it. It was not quite the traditional office interview across the top of a desk, but a sort of gentler version of it. Above all, from Hurst's point of view, it was not in the vicarage, with Christabel's room and its great sofa down at the end of a side passage. He felt quite confident that Christabel did not know of the meeting at all. All the same, she made her presence felt. The meeting was between priest and layman, but also between man and man.

Richards said, 'Now – do you want to tell me, or would you rather I asked you questions? I ask, because in my experience question and answer is much the more effective procedure. Nobody gets left behind. Also, oddly enough, most people prefer it. It is difficult enough to talk straight, without having to decide for yourself how to set about it.'

'Question me, by all means. If I cannot answer your question, I'll say so. If I can, I'll try to answer truthfully. But as you say yourself, this is not the confessional, and I am entitled to my reservations. If you find you cannot help me within these terms of reference, that is my risk.'

Richards sat back and smiled. 'For a man seeking guidance in spiritual distress,' he said, 'you are very peremptory and matter-of-fact. You have a good brain, of course, and a professional ability with the language. Yet I am convinced the distress is there.' He leant forward again, looking, not at Hurst, but at his hands clasped on the table in front of him. 'Tell me,' he said, 'leaving aside for the moment the actual subject of your distress, what made you decide to ask me about it?'

'In the first place, you yourself suggested the possibility when we talked the other evening. In the second, I do regard you, whatever you may say, as a man in authority. By this I mean that you have conviction and certainty where I have only doubt. I cannot share the source of your conviction, but I respect the conviction itself. I suppose I envy it. Doubters always do, I think, however much they parade their liberty.'

Richards looked up at him and smiled. It was a gentle, almost rueful, smile, that sat strangely on the handsome determined face. 'My dear chap,' he said, 'do you think I don't have my doubts? The difference is that I can leave mine to God, as you cannot. What I have isn't conviction, it's faith. If you come to me as a sort of superman, you're going to be disappointed. At best I'm only a mouthpiece.'

For a moment they looked at each other. The silence in the church was as palpable as a presence. Hurst said, 'There is another thing. After I had talked to you the other evening, I had the first full night's sleep I had had for a very long time. When I woke, I had – I don't know, I had the feeling that in my sleep I had had the answer. Or at least the inkling of an answer. I could not grasp it with my waking mind, but the effect of it stayed with me, and gave me extraordinary relief. It did not last, but I did have it.'

Richards was looking at his hands again. It occurred to

Hurst what beautiful hands they were, beautiful but very strong and capable. The face bent over then was full of concentration and very serious. Finally Richards nodded. He said, 'Can you connect this – this feeling you had with any particular thing we had said?'

'Not really. But I think it was something to do with love.'

Quite suddenly, Richards threw back his head and laughed. It was a startling sound in the enormous silence, but he did not explain his laughter. He said, 'That it might well be. All right. Now let's think about the thing itself. You talked just now of an answer. That implies a problem. You being the man you are, I think it would be a practical problem. Is that right?'

'Yes. I need to do something. I cannot bear not to. But I don't know what to do.'

Richards nodded. 'How long have you had this problem?'

'I suppose in effect for the last five years. But the need to find a solution has only gradually become apparent. At first I was hardly aware that the problem was there.'

For a moment the two men looked at each other. Then Richards said, 'I think you were last here five years ago?'

'Yes.'

'And the problem arose then?'

'In effect, yes.'

'And you came back here, consciously or unconsciously, to seek a solution?'

'Consciously, but not very coherently. I had found no solution anywhere else.'

'I see.' Richards lent forward over the table again. His mouth was set now and his forehead slightly creased. When he spoke again, his eyes came up to meet Hurst's, but he did not move his head, so that he looked up at him from under his brows. He looked suddenly more human, but also

74

more formidable. He said, 'Something when you were here before. I take it from what you have said so far that you do not wish to tell me what it was. But the fact that it had happened gradually made it necessary that you should take some further step. Would the necessity be an external or an internal one, practical or mental?'

'Internal and mental. But it had its practical aspect. I found I could no longer work.'

'So ultimately you came back here, where the original cause had arisen, in the hope – a rather incoherent hope, you say – that you might be able, here, to take the further action that seemed needed?'

'Yes. I can't pretend that the thing went as clearly as that in my mind. But I think that states the position. At any rate, I found I had to come back.'

'Then what is your problem? And how can I help you with it when you are unable to tell me the facts that gave rise to it?'

'I think my problem is this. The need to act is, as I said, an internal need. To act would help no one but myself. Now that I have come back, I have come to see that, whatever it did for me, it would almost certainly hurt other people. There is a clash between my interest, if it is my interest, and theirs. If I could find a way that would help me without hurting them, I should have my solution, but I have not found it.'

Richards raised his head again, and once more the two men looked at each other in silence. Then he said, 'This need of yours – leaving aside for a moment the practical need to continue your work – is a mental need. I shall assume that it is what I should call a crisis of conscience. How great is it? Can you say it is intolerable?'

'I have at times considered killing myself to escape from it.'

Richards threw himself back in his chair and brought both hands on to the table with a thud. It was as sudden and startling in its way as his laugh had been, but now he was angry. He said, 'You must not consider that in any circumstances. Leaving aside the Christian arguments, which you may not recognise, you must realise that to do that would hurt other people too. I cannot say whom or how much. But someone certainly. I have never known a suicide that didn't. That is no solution at all. That is one thing I can tell you, with all the force and conviction there is in me. You say you have come to me for guidance. Will you accept my judgement on that at least?'

Hurst said, 'I don't want to kill myself. I am not at all sure, when it came to the point, I should have the courage to do it. If there is a suicidal type, I don't think I conform to it. All right, let's rule that out. I told you I had considered it because you asked me the extent of my need to find a way out.'

'Good. That is something gained at least.' Richards still sat back in his chair, but now he sank his chin on his chest and sat staring in front of him. His anger had passed, but his face looked drawn and unhappy. When he spoke, he spoke very quietly. He said, 'There is a specifically Christian solution to your difficulty. You should confess and seek absolution and do whatever penance was fitting. But it seems the mercy of God is of no use to you. It is your own forgiveness you want.' He lapsed into thought again. Then he lifted his head and looked at Hurst. 'Then I think all I can tell you is that you must learn to live with your burden, whatever it is. You cannot seek peace at the expense of other people. My ability to give you practical advice is limited by my ignorance of the facts. But I should say get away from here for a start, now you have learnt what you have by coming here. Go away and do not come back. If you cannot do your proper work, find other work which will occupy you and give you a living. Hard physical work, for choice. You live too much in your own mind. Leaving aside all idea of penance, the exhaustion of the body is the greatest settler of the mind. I can see no other solution.'

The silence came down then and shut them in. They sat drooped on their hard chairs in the little lamplit enclosure while the great stone spaces darkened over it. Something had gone wrong. Whatever he had expected, Hurst knew that there had at some point been a failure, and that Charles Richards was as conscious of it as he himself was. After a bit he gathered his feet under him, ready to get up and go. But he did not want to go, because there was nothing outside for him to go to. He said, 'Your answer is that there is no solution.'

Richards said, 'In human terms I do not think there is. People in your sort of case are always looking for miracles, but they want them on easy terms. Like Macbeth, you know:

"Canst thou not minister to a mind diseased,
    Pluck from the memory a rooted sorrow,
    Raze out the written troubles of the brain,
    And with some sweet oblivious antidote
    Cleanse the stuffed bosom of that perilous stuff
    Which weighs upon the heart?"

It's not grace and mercy he's asking for. It's patent medicine. A sweet oblivious antidote. The doctor's at least honest. He's a humanist, of course, like all the rest of them. But at least he knows the limitations of humanism. He says, "Therein the patient must minister to himself." It's no good to Macbeth, but at least it's honest.'

It was Richards who got up first. He pulled himself to his

feet slowly, as if he was lifting a weight which, for all his physical strength, he found it hard to lift. When he was up, he squared his shoulders, and stood there looking down at Hurst in his chair. He made no further movement at all, but there was no irresolution in it. It was a conscious and maintained immobility. But Hurst did not move either. He sat there, leaning forward a little and gazing down at the worn carpet in front of him. Finally Richards said, 'I do not say there is no solution. All I say is that on your terms of reference I cannot suggest one. I have told you two things you must not do. Perhaps really it is only one thing, at least from your point of view. You must not think of killing yourself, and you must not allow yourself, in your struggle to escape, to hurt other people. So far as I can understand it, I don't think your attitude is by any means wholly wrong. Much better feel as you do than remain unaware of the dilemma. But I think there is more than a touch of self-indulgence in it. That is why it is particularly important that you should go out of your way to consider the effect on other people of whatever you decide to do. Other people are always the most important factor, even if you exclude God. As you said just now, it is something to do with love.' He smiled, and Hurst, looking up, caught the smile, and found something like a very gentle mockery in it. He got up too.

He said, 'I'm grateful to you. Please believe that. I'm not sure, yet, quite what it is I'm grateful for, but I am grateful.' He smiled back at Richard's smile. There was no hint of mockery in either smile now, but both were a little rueful. He said, 'I hope I haven't made you late for your appointment.'

'No, no. There is still time. You go along now, and I'll shut up here. I'll see you again, I expect.'

'You do?'

Richards nodded. 'I am fairly sure of it,' he said.

Hurst nodded too. He opened the door in the screen. The church was not really dark, except by contrast with the yellow glow behind him. He tiptoed across to the great south door and let himself out into the evening daylight.

IX

Lizz said, 'Mike? Mike, can I come in? I knocked, but you didn't hear. I knew you were in because I saw the lights. Mike, are you all right?'

Hurst pulled himself half out of his chair, but she pushed him back into it. She sat on the arm, looking down at him. He said, 'Sorry, Lizz. I didn't mean – Yes, I'm all right.'

'You don't look it,' she said. 'Did you hear me knock, in fact?'

His eyes dropped under her intense stare, and his head went forward on to his chest. He sat slumped in the chair as he had been sitting before she came. He did not know how long he had been sitting like that. He did not think it was very long. He said, 'Yes, I was going to – Nothing personal, Lizz. I knew it was you, of course. No one else knocks like that. Only —'

'Only you couldn't rouse yourself?'

'Something like that.'

She did not say anything; but she put out a hand and very gently touched the top of his head. It was not quite a pat and not quite a stroke. The finger tips came down one after the other in a line across his head, so that there was a feeling of motion, but in fact they did not move. They rested lightly for a moment and then she took her hand away. It was a gentler version of what her hand did on the panel of the front door. He was reminded, suddenly and incongruously, of Christabel's fevered fingers on his arms and body. Women's fingers, he thought. Perhaps there was not so much incongruity after all, only a matter of application and control. She said, 'I met your Christabel today. For the first time, in fact. It seems funny when I felt I knew her so well.'

His head came up at that, and they looked at each other. They were both very serious. 'Did you?' he said. 'How did that happen?'

'It was her doing. She came to the office. I knew she was coming, of course. Nothing important – just something to do with her money. I don't see in the visitors. Jane does that. I'm the inside girl. It was old Morris she was seeing. He always deals with the quality. I heard her say good-bye to him and the door of his room shut, and then the door of my room opened and there she was, looking in at me. We didn't pretend not to know each other, of course. She said – I forget how she put it, but something about our getting to know each other. She did it very prettily, I must say. Anyway, she said would I come out and have coffee with her. I get my break, of course, and there is nothing to stop me going out if I want to. So I said yes, and we went to the coffee-shop place, and she stood me treat. We talked nonstop. No difficulty at all. All girls together, you know?'

Hurst smiled at her, but he was conscious of a faint feeling of disquiet. He did not connect it with the way Christabel had watched him and Charles over the coffee tray as they came in from the dining-room. He had been on the other end of the experience then, and it did not occur to him that the experience was the same. Neither sex can ever quite get over this suspicion of divided allegiances, but neither expects the other to feel the same. He said, 'What did you talk about, then?'

She smiled back at him. They were not at all in the mood for archness, and she did not say 'Not you, anyhow,' but she wanted to reassure him. She said, 'Oh – everything and nothing. You never come to the point when you're being vetted. That's not the technique.'

'But you felt you were being vetted?'

'Oh yes. We both were, if it comes to that. She started it, of course, because it was easier for her, but it was fifty-fifty. By the end, anyway. That would be one of the things she'd want to find out.'

He accepted the re-assurance she offered him, but found in it fresh cause for disquiet. If it was not two women against him, it was Christabel against him and Lizz. He said, 'Why should she want to vet you, Lizz? Vet you for what? You've both been here all this time.'

'You haven't.'

He was on the point of saying, 'What have I got to do with it?' but did not say it. He did not in fact know, or not at all clearly, but he did not want to hear Lizz's explanation. For a moment he said nothing and she noted his silence but did not comment on it. Finally he said, 'Well, what did you make of each other?'

'It was all right,' she said. 'I told you, we got on like a house on fire.'

'I know you got on. But that was part of the vetting process. You said so yourself. What conclusion did you reach?'

Lizz thought for a bit. She still sat on the arm of his chair, but now she turned a little away from him. 'I like her,' she said, 'that's the funny thing. I've been hating her guts all this time, and when I met her, I liked her. There's a lot of niceness in her.'

'There had to be. You don't know Charles Richards. All the same, you should have known enough about him to know he wouldn't pick up a floosey, even a shiny, well-heeled one, if that's how you saw her.'

'All right,' she said. 'I was prejudiced. Good God, I don't deny that. She's not a floosey, not even a floosey playing it careful. Suppose you tell me how nice she is.'

'I thought you were going to tell me.'

They were sparring now. They were much less serious than they had been, but the sympathy between them had gone. She said, 'You tell me, and I'll tell you how right you are.'

'Well – she's a pretty complicated person. Of course, most people are when you get to know them. But there's a very deep division here. A light side and a dark side. The light side is the real one. That's the one you liked. It knows all about the division and isn't very happy about it. Does that make sense to you?'

She had turned to him again now and was looking down at him. 'Oh yes,' she said. 'It's not all that uncommon, anyway. Not in women. Men are much more of a piece. But go on.'

'Well, that's it, really. When I was here before, I saw mainly the dark side. I don't know whose fault that was. Mine as well as hers, I expect. Anyway, it played hell with me. You know that. Now I'm different. The thing burnt itself out. To some extent, so's she different. That would be mostly Charles's doing, I think. He'd see the light side, of course, in her and in everybody.'

'Only the light side?'

'I shouldn't think so. He's too good for that. I don't know, of course. But for him it would be the light side that mattered, and so far as Christabel's concerned, he's right.'

'What about you, then?'

'I see both. But then I already know the dark side is there. More to the point, she knows I know. She doesn't have to pretend with me, any more than she does with herself.'

She looked down at him sombrely. All the lightness of touch had gone, and she was in deadly earnest again. She said, 'When doesn't she have to pretend? I didn't know you were seeing all that much of her.'

'Once only, since the dinner-party, I mean. By pure chance and in quite extraordinary circumstances.'

She kept her fierce, concentrated stare on his face, but he shook his head at her. He was giving nothing more away. After a bit she said, 'And she didn't pretend then?'

He shook his head again. Then, as with a conscious effort, he took his eyes off the wide blue eyes above him, and his face turned forward and downward again. He spoke very quietly. He said, 'She didn't pretend, nor did I, but we were on contrary courses. I don't think either of us behaved very well. I know I didn't. But it was an impossible situation – which, as I say, neither of us had sought.' He hesitated, struggling with himself, struggling with his nagging need to tell somebody, at least to tell somebody something and not carry it all inside himself. He said, 'I hit her, Lizz. God help me, I hit her. I was angry and in a panic. But it wasn't really her I was angry with, it was myself. It always is. But I didn't hit myself, I hit her.'

She had made a small, sudden sound, almost a yelp, as if it was she who had been hit, suddenly and unexpectedly. She said, 'Mike, how could you?' He said nothing, and after a bit she said, 'Mike, don't you see? If I did that to you, and you hit me, I'd deserve it, but not Christabel.'

His head came up with a jerk and they stared at each other. Her eyes were no longer fierce, but her mouth was drawn down hard.

'You?' he said, and she nodded, very slowly.

'Me,' she said. 'Does that surprise you?'

He looked away again, almost afraid of what he saw. 'I don't know,' he said. 'I hadn't thought —' He did not say what it was he had not thought. He was not sure he knew. He was out of his depth altogether.

She said, 'Mike.' She said it very quietly, almost in a

84

whisper. He turned his face up to her, and very slowly her face came down over his, and her mouth on to his mouth. Her lips were very soft and warm and a little tremulous. He was shaken suddenly by an enormous upthrust of desire, such as he had not known through all these tormented years. He half turned as he sat, but now her mouth was gone from his, and she was sitting back on the arm of his chair again, very close beside him, but out of reach. She spoke again almost in a whisper, looking away from him. She said, 'Now do you see?'

His mouth was dry. He said, 'Lizz —,' but she put a hand on his arm, compelling him to silence.

She said, 'Do you think I haven't got my dark side, if that's what you call it? It's in the blood, this thing. Good God, look at Mum. What do you think keeps John Merrow hanging around as he does? He can't like being where he is. But he can't break himself clear, don't you see? And look at me. I'm like Mum, aren't I? Physically, I mean. My body, not my face. My face is Dad's, I suppose, and he was a right bastard by all accounts. That's where the hardness comes from. Mum isn't hard at all. But at least the hardness keeps the rest of the works in order. I know what I want and I can wait for it. I've been lucky that far. Christabel probably never did know. I doubt if she does now. That's what I meant when I said that if you hit me, I'd deserve it. But you mustn't hit her. It isn't fair.'

She got up then and went across to the chair opposite his. She was wearing something dark and soft and close-fitting, and every rounded surface showed as she moved. She looked terribly mature for her age. Her skin would be white all over, and if she let it down, her dark hair would come down to the small of her back. He saw her suddenly as the typist turned mother-goddess, and knew he had been right to be frightened of her. Only when she turned and looked at

85

him the blue eyes and the set of the mouth belied the picture. Dad's face, she had said, and Dad had been a right bastard, as his son had been after him. But her face was not like Jack's at all. Even the eyes were different. He said, 'All the same, you don't know what she did to me, Lizz. Maybe she couldn't help herself, but it happened to me, all the same. Maybe the cat can't, but that doesn't help the mouse.'

She said, 'What did happen, then?'

'We made love once, quite early on. After that, nothing. She wouldn't have it.'

She nodded. 'That was bad,' she said. 'I can see that. All the same, you got away. She let you go. If I had you, I'd never let you go.'

'At a price,' he said. 'I got away, but at a price. I'm still paying, Lizz.'

She got up then, a little impatiently. 'I can't understand that,' she said. 'You've got to stop paying some time. Everybody does. Some never pay at all. Jack's never paid for anything in his life. I shouldn't think Dad did, either. I don't know about me, not yet. I've got a lot of Mum in me. But I don't intend to pay more than I can help.'

He got up too. 'No,' he said. 'I don't think you can understand.' They looked at each other for a moment. Then she turned and went to the door. 'Give me time, Lizz,' he said, and she turned again.

'You can have all the time you want,' she said. 'I've told you that. You must make your own decision. After that I can help you, but you must decide first.' She turned and went out of the door, and he stood there in the middle of the room, watching the door as she shut it behind her.

It was later, when he was in the kitchen, that someone knocked on the back door. He thought at once of John Merrow. He hoped it was him. He did not know what he could say to him, but he would be very glad to see him. But the knock did not sound like him. There was something hurried and uncertain about it, and John always seemed to know what he was doing and take his time about doing it. He dried his hands on the roller-towel and went to the door. It was Mrs. Basset. She had a dark coat on and a scarf over her head. It was dark outside now, but she had a torch in her hand. She stood there, looking at him doubtfully in the light from the door. He said, 'Hullo, Mrs. Basset. Anything wrong?' He did not ask her to come in, because he did not think that that was what she wanted.

She said, 'Nothing wrong, Mr. Hurst. Can I come in a minute?'

He stood back, feeling a little guilty and apprehensive, though he could not tell why. 'Of course,' he said. 'I'm so sorry. I thought perhaps there was something you wanted me to do.'

She came in, slipping the scarf back off her head. She took the scarf off and rolled it up neatly, and put it in one pocket of her coat and the torch in the other. She loosened her coat but did not take it off. She looked at Hurst all the time, and he at her, both a little uneasy. He noticed for the first time how sleek and fine her hair was and how well she carried herself. It had not occurred to him before to think of her as attractive or unattractive, because she had no attraction for him. Now, after what Lizz had said, he saw in her all the marks of a woman who has always thought of herself as attractive and sees no reason in middle age to alter her way of thinking. He said, 'Come into the sitting-room. I'd just finished here.'

She took her eyes off his and took a quick look round the kitchen, the look no woman with a house of her own can ever help giving at a kitchen run by a man. She said, 'Well, I'd just as soon stay here. I won't keep you a moment.'

Hurst pulled out the two kitchen chairs from the table, and they sat down on them, looking at each other across the newly wiped table top. She said, 'It's about Elizabeth.'

87

Hurst said, 'She was here not long ago. Hasn't she come back?'

His voice showed his concern, and she looked at him curiously. 'Oh yes, Mr. Hurst. She came straight back. I knew she was up here, of course. But she was upset when she come in. I wondered – well, the fact is, I wondered if you knew how it was with her. You've always been friends with her, I know that, right from when she was just a child, but she's grown up now and sees things different. I'd better tell you straight, she's very much in love with you. The truth is I'm afraid what you might do to her. I don't mean mucking about with her, getting her pregnant and all that. You wouldn't do that, neither of you. But I mean, if you're going to go off some time and leave her here, the sooner you go the better, so as she can start thinking of someone else.' She stopped, looking at him a little apprehensively. 'I hope you'll excuse me talking so straight,' she said, 'but she's the only decent child I've got, and I don't want her life mucked up like mine was.' For a moment neither of them said anything. Then she said, 'She doesn't know I'm here, of course. There'd be a fine old row if she did.'

Hurst said, 'Good lord, I know that. Look, Mrs. Basset, I want to be straight with you, as you've been with me, but I'm damned if I know what to say. I know Lizz is – fond of me, of course. She's made no bones about it. I'm very fond of her too, you know, and God knows I don't want her hurt any more than you do. Only – well, I'm in a bit of a mess myself at the moment. I don't know what to do, about Lizz or anything else.'

She looked at him very squarely. She said, 'I don't know anything about your troubles, Mr. Hurst, and I don't want to. They're no business of mine. But Elizabeth is. All I'm asking is that you should consider her a bit as well as yourself.'

88

He looked at her with such desperate unhappiness in his face that her own face softened, and she made a little involuntary clucking sound, as if she would come to him and comfort him too if she could. He said, 'Don't you think Lizz can look after herself to some extent, Mrs. Basset? She's got a tough streak in her, you know. More than either you or I have. She says it's her father in her. I never knew him, of course.'

Mrs. Basset said very quietly, 'My husband was the hardest man I ever knew. I was afraid of him nearly all the time. We all were, even Jack, right up to the day he died. Maybe she has got a tough streak in her, as you say. But it's not helping her now. It just makes her more determined. She's the sort to put all her eggs in one basket. It's all or nothing with her. When that sort fall, they fall hard.'

He said nothing, because he could find nothing to say, and she got up. 'I won't keep you,' she said. 'I've said what I come to say. I don't think there's any harm in you, Mr. Hurst. I don't want you to think that. Only I wanted to make sure you knew what you were doing, so far as Elizabeth's concerned. You think about it. I know you'll do the best you can. Now I'll be going.' She took her scarf out of her pocket and put it over head. He got up then and went to the door and opened it for her.

He said, 'Thank you for coming, Mrs. Basset. Let me think about it. I promise I'll do the best I can.'

She put out a hand and touched him lightly on the arm that held the door. 'That's right,' she said. 'Good night, then, Mr. Hurst.'

He said, 'Good night, Mrs. Basset,' and shut the door quietly after her. Then he went back and sat down again on his chair by the kitchen table. After a bit he put his elbows on the table and leant his head on his hands. For a long time he did not move.

X

The key of the shed hung on a nail over the draining-board of the sink. He saw it every time he washed up. He had put it there just before he left and had not touched it since he came back. There was nothing in the shed he ever wanted now. The key did not worry him much. It worried him a good deal less than several other things did when he was at the sink. There was very little reason why it should worry him at all, but then there was no apparent reason whatever why some of the others should. His worries lay about in odd corners of his mind, ready to spring up and jab him when he tripped on the right wires, but he could never see the wire before he tripped on it. Today, when he had finished at the sink and hung the tea-towel up to dry, he stretched out a hand on an impulse and took the key off its nail.

He thought he knew what was in the shed and where it all was, but he felt he ought to go and look at it because it was the only part of the buildings he had not looked at since he came back. It would make something to do, and the shed was neutral. There might even be something there which he had forgotten, and which it might please him to find again. Small inexplicable pleasures of this sort did occur, though not nearly so often as the inexplicable griefs. He went out of the back door and walked across to the shed. It was fastened with a padlock on a staple and hasp. The lock was a galvanised iron one which did not mind the weather, and the key turned easily enough. The hinges of the door complained a little, and there were cobwebs festooned across the doorway, but otherwise there did not seem to be anything wrong. The shed was dry and, with the sun on it, already slightly warm. He brushed the cobwebs aside with his hand and went inside.

There were no surprises, except the mild general surprise of seeing it all again. That was simply a delayed part of the surprise he had felt when he first came back, the surprise of finding that everything had gone on existing without him. The things had gone on existing without change, except the trees in the wood, which had grown. The people had gone on existing too, but had changed as much as he had. He had been surprised at the changes in the people and at the lack of change in the things. He knew that neither was reasonable, but he had felt it all the same. In any case, there was nothing to do in the shed, though he was glad he had looked at it and found it all in order. He came out again and locked the door. It was only as he was walking back to the house that he wondered about the spade. It was as he had left it, clean and slightly oiled, only he had an idea he had left it on the other side of the shed. It was on the left of the shed now, the side nearer the house, and he thought it had been on the right. He remembered putting the spade away very clearly, but he might be wrong about where he had put it. In any case, the thing did not engage his mind for more than a moment. He walked to the back door with the key in his hand, and as he got there he saw a car on the side road below the back of the house.

He knew the car at once, and stopped to see what it would do. He stood there against the back of the cottage, as the car came down the road towards the gate. He could not see through the reflected light on the windscreen, but the driver could see him if she looked up. He did not wave or make any sign of recognition, but he looked at the car, so that if she saw him at all, she would know he had seen it. The car came along slowly, so slowly that he thought for a moment that it was going to stop, but it did not stop. It went slowly past the gate and disappeared under the curve of the hill.

He was worried and did not know what to do. If Christabel had come this way at all, and by that road, it must be something to do with him. It could not be Lizz she was coming to see, not at this hour. She would have come in the hope of finding him in, or in the hope of finding him not in, or merely to see if he was there or not. Maybe she did not know what she had come for, with the car going as hesitantly as that, but it would still be him she was hesitating about. And he felt guilty about her, doubly guilty since Lizz's rebuke. He could not bear the thought of her driving slowly past, wanting to see him but not wanting to come up to the house. The fact that she had almost certainly seen him, and knew that he had seen her, made it worse. He did not think he could actively seek a meeting with her, because it must be for her to decide. But in case she did want to see him, he could not just sit inside the house and wait for her to come up. That would be cruel, and ten to one she would not do it.

He went into the kitchen and put the key back on its nail. Then he went out of the back door again, and began walking down the drive to the gate. He could not miss her this way, not if she came back at all. The one thing he was certain of was that she would not come up the path in front of the cottage. He thought if he went down on to the road and walked there on the straight stretch past the gate, she would be bound to see him if she did come back. Then it would be up to her. If she wanted to speak to him, she could stop and perhaps pick him up. If not, she could drive past, wave to him, perhaps, to cover the formalities, but still drive on. When he came to the road he looked southwards along it, but there was nothing in sight. Then he turned and started walking northwards, with the cottage and, so far as he knew, the car behind him. He walked steadily, but as slowly as he decently could without looking as if he was waiting for something. He did not know what he would do when he came to the bend of the road, where he would pass out of sight of the gate, but he would decide that when he got there.

He was nearly there when he heard a car on the road behind him. He could not tell if it was her car, and he was not going to turn round, but if it was, she would have seen him by now. He walked on, a little more purposefully now, in case it was not her at all. He walked until he heard the car slowing down behind him, and turned his head only as it came alongside. He and the car stopped together. The nearside window was shut and he could not speak through it. He opened the door and looked in at her as she sat at the wheel. He thought she looked pale, self-possessed but not happy. He smiled at her and said, 'Hullo, Christabel,' and after a moment she smiled back.

She said, 'I wondered —' but he cut her off short to save explanations.

'May I get in?' he said. She nodded, and he got in beside her, and the car moved off.

Once the car was moving, she never took her eyes off the road ahead. After a bit she said, 'It was nice of you to come down.'

'It seemed best,' he said, and she nodded.

The car moved on steadily and still all he saw of her was her profile. Then she said, 'I wanted —' and he said, 'I want —' almost simultaneously. They both stopped. He laughed, and she gave him a quick sideways glance. When she looked ahead again, he could see that she was just smiling, but it looked a rather uncertain smile. He said, 'You wanted to explain something or apologise. I wanted to explain and apologise. We both wanted to apologise for something which we agreed had never happened. Is that it?'

She nodded. 'I suppose so. It did happen, all the same.' He took breath to speak, but she said, 'No, let me finish. It's what I came for.' She thought for a bit. Then she said, 'It was a pretty appalling coincidence, after all. I hadn't been to the house for quite a long time. I used to at first, but not for some time now. I suppose it was seeing you that started me off again. Not – not you in particular, really, but I told you – you brought things back, simply by being here. And then Charles was away those few days, and there was that half-moon, and I couldn't help myself, and I went back. Simply to the place, I mean. I don't know why, really. The old thing about murderers going back, I suppose. I didn't come to you, after all. It wasn't particularly you I was thinking about, even though you had come back. And then there you were, waiting for me in the trees. It was too much. It threw me clean off balance. I'm sorry, Mike. That's all.'

He said, 'I understand, Christabel. Really I think I do understand. But whatever happened to you couldn't justify my doing what I did. It was panic, you know, in a way. I was off balance, too. But the moment you'd gone I felt bad about it, and I've felt bad ever since. I'd have come after you if I could, just to say so.'

She shook her head. 'It was anger,' she said. 'It was the best thing you could have done. Standard shock treatment, after all, in cases of self-induced hysteria. And better than derision, don't you see? Anything's better than that. If you had laughed at me, I think I really should have gone home and taken an over-dose. So there's no need to feel too sorry about what you did, even if it didn't strike you as particularly noble at the time.'

The car had come out on to high ground, and she pulled it off the road on to a patch of grass with a wide landscape in front of them. He knew the hill, but could not remember its name. They both sat there silent, staring out over the great stretch of green country. There was nothing particularly picturesque about it. Standard English country, but at this time of the year near enough paradise for ordinary consumption. They did not take much notice of it.

She said, 'I'm glad it happened, in a way. I can talk to you now. There's nothing left I mustn't say. And I need someone I can talk to like that.'

'I don't think I'm very well qualified as a consultant.'

'You don't need any qualifications, except to know, and you do know. You needn't say anything, really. Only listen.'

He nodded. 'I'll listen, then,' he said, but for a long time she did not say anything.

At last she said, 'I'm frightened, Mike. Not just about – this thing you know about. Or not directly. It's more practical than that. More solid, anyhow. And more frightening.' She looked at him for a moment, and then looked away again. 'I'm frightened about Jack Basset,' she said.

He did not move or say anything. She had told him he need not speak, and he did not. She took a deep breath, like someone about to dive into cold water. 'It happened with him, too, you know. Just once. Right at the end, just before he went away. He came – he said he had come to say goodbye. I suppose that helped, his saying he was going off for good and not coming back. What frightens me now is that he might.' He still did not say anything. 'Jack's a bad person,' she said. 'As bad as any person I've ever met. I can trust you. I couldn't trust him at all. No one could. There were others, quite a long time ago now. But they're all – I don't have to be afraid of any of them. It's Jack I'm afraid of.'

He said, 'Do you think he could really do any harm, even if he did come back?'

95

'I think he'd try. It might not do him any good, but I think he'd try, just for the fun of it.'

He thought for a bit. Then he said, 'But Christabel, it's a matter of trusting Charles, isn't it? So long as you could trust Charles, Jack could do you no harm. And you could trust Charles. You know that.'

All this time she did not look at him. She sat staring out over the fields and trees, frowning slightly, as if she was trying to outface whatever it was she saw in her mind's eye. At last she said, 'I've got to trust myself, too, haven't I? And I don't, Mike, how can I? Jack knows too much. He's one of the ones who do. And he wouldn't slap my face for me. I could trust Charles with the past, before I knew him. Whatever it did to him, I could trust him with it. But not with that.'

He had made up his mind now. He sat up decisively and put out a hand and touched her arm. 'Look, Christabel,' he said, 'I'll tell you what I think, and I'm fairly sure I'm right. If Jack were to come back, you should go to Charles at once and tell him – tell him you're afraid of Jack. You needn't say more, and he wouldn't make you. Once you'd told him, half the fear would have gone. But I don't think Jack will come back. No one does think so, not even his own family. He meant to go for good and he went. There are people here he wouldn't be keen to meet, you know. Plenty of them, I shouldn't wonder. I don't think he'll be back. You must just cling on to that, and in time you'll forget he ever existed. Can you do that?'

She drew a long breath and nodded. 'All right,' she said. 'Thank you, Mike. Now shall I drive you back?'

'Not all the way. I could do with a walk anyway. Get me down on to the Frantham road and I'll walk from there.'

She nodded again and started the car. She backed it on to the road and drove back the way they had come. They did not say anything more to each other until they came to the road. Then she stopped the car but left the engine running. He got out and they looked at each other through the open door. She said, 'I can trust you, Mike, can't I?'

'More than you think,' he said. Then he shut the door, and she drove off towards Frantham. He watched the car for a moment and then turned and walked off the other way. He wondered how far he had committed himself, and to what, and how far he could trust himself. There was too much trusting going on in all directions, and somebody some time was going to give way.

He saw the wood before he recognised it and before he realised that he was, even at this distance, within sight of home. It stood up dressed in its new leaf, a hummock of pale green against the pale blue sky. There was a lot of country, undulating in short slopes, and a lot of trees still between them, but the wood stood clear of it all. It was getting to be quite a landmark. There were still hedgerow trees in this country of small fields, but very little woodland. One of these days they would be putting a preservation order on it. It was a thought, certainly. For a moment he found himself smiling, and wondered what he was at. John Merrow had said something about keeping the wood when he had asked about buying the cottage. He had not thought much of it at the time, because he had not really let himself consider selling, but now he wondered about that, too.

It was only when he came round the last bend of the road that he saw the cottage itself. It was a pretty place, as John had said. Not so pretty perhaps from this side, because you could see the outbuildings, and they had few architectural pretensions. All the same, it made a pleasant group, squeezed on to its corner of the small steep hill, with the wood covering all the rest of the top. It would fetch a very high price these days in the open market. He wondered whether John had considered this when he had said he could give him a fair price for it. It would be a lot of money for a man like that to find, and he wondered if he really had it and if so, where he had got it. But then he knew very little about John altogether, and he did not see him making an offer he could not sustain. He trusted John, instinctively but completely. More trusting, but John was a better man to trust than he was.

He went on walking, steadily but reluctantly, with his eyes on the cottage. He never wanted to go back to it when he was away from it, and never wanted to go out of it when he was once inside. He hated the place, but he was tied to it. He could not leave it, but he could not live there always, and he hated the flat too. He did not know what he could do.

XI

John Merrow said, 'There was a chap up here just now. Did you see him?'

'No,' said Hurst. 'What sort of a chap? What was he doing?'

'Just hanging around. Looking to see if there was anyone here. Don't know who he was. He didn't say.'

'You spoke to him, then?'

'Oh yes. He came to me first. Well, to Amy's, I suppose, really, but there was only me there. She's over at the house.'

'What did he want, then?'

'He was asking for Jack. Asking about him, anyway. I don't think he expected to find him here, not by the way he talked. Anyway, I couldn't tell him anything, so he came on up here. But you weren't here, you say.'

'No, I've just come in from the back. Was he here long?'

'Not long, no. Only I saw him hanging about, and I reckoned you couldn't be in, so after a bit I thought I'd come up, just to see. But now I find you're back and he's gone. You didn't see him, though?'

'No. I shouldn't have, if he'd gone the front way. He couldn't have got into the house, anyway. It was locked.'

'That's all right, then. Mind you, I don't know there was any harm in him. Only he didn't say who he was, and I wondered.'

Hurst thought for a bit. Then he said, 'Do you get many like that?'

'What, asking for Jack? Not now, we don't. We used to at one time, after he first went. We even had the police once. He owed a bit around the place, I think. And there was a girl that would have liked to get him up before the magistrates, if she could. More than one, from what I heard. He had a way of getting what he wanted from the women. Seems to have, anyhow. You wouldn't think so to look at him. Not my taste, but you never know what they'll like, some of them.'

'I was asked,' Hurst said. 'Just after I got back. About a car he hadn't paid for, and then sold before he left.'

'That's right. I heard about that.' He looked at Hurst for a moment and then shook his head. 'No,' he said. 'Jack meant to go, all right, and he didn't mean to come back. There's a few that would like to get their hands on him, still are, apparently, but apart from that, I wouldn't say he's missed. None of us down there want him back, anyway. Not even Amy, though she won't say so. She had enough from his father without having it all over again from Master Jack. As for me – well, you can imagine, me being where I am. But then I've told you about that.' He waited again, but Hurst said nothing. Then he said, 'Look, Mr. Hurst, can I come in for a moment? I don't want to stand talking out here.'

He had come round from the front of the house and found Hurst in the kitchen with the back door open. They had been talking through the open door ever since, but now Hurst said, 'All right, John,' and turned and led the way into the sitting-room. He sat down and pointed Merrow to the chair opposite. 'Well?' he said.

Merrow said, 'Well, I wondered if you'd been thinking any more about what we talked about the last time I was up here. About letting me have this place, I mean. But there's more I wanted to say than that. The truth is, whoever you sell it to, it's time you went. That's for your own sake and everyone else's. We all think that. You're doing yourself no good hanging about here like this, you're not getting your work done and you're getting yourself talked about. One of these days, if you don't make up your mind to go, you'll be doing something silly, something everyone will be sorry for and you'll be sorry for yourself before you're more than a day or two older. I've told you I want this place for myself. So I do, only I reckoned you might let me have it when perhaps you wouldn't want anyone else to. But so far as I'm concerned, I wouldn't mind who had it so long as you'd make up your mind once for all to be finished with it.'

He had talked himself on to his feet, a big man and very strong, standing almost over Hurst as he sat in his chair and looked up at him. There was no menace in him, only a sort of desperate determination to go through with what he had probably had no clear intention of starting. There was no resentment in Hurst either. He saw Merrow less as a person than as an embodiment of one of the arguments that went on in his own mind. All the same, he was a person, and one he liked and trusted, and that gave the familiar argument an unfamiliar force. He said, 'Who's talking about me, John?'

Merrow made a sudden sweeping gesture with his hand. 'Well – everyone,' he said. 'You know what it is in a small place. Nothing unkind, but they think you're acting queer, and they don't like it. They're not making anything of it – not yet. But they will if you go on. There'll always be somebody will think up an explanation, right or wrong, and it won't be one you'd like. They're not unkind round here, but if anyone goes on the way you're going, the reasons people think up aren't going to be nice ones. You know that.'

Hurst was not looking at him now. He sat staring at the floor in front of him. His face was its accustomed blank, but his mind was in a turmoil. Merrow did not move or speak. The birds sang in the wood, and in one of the fields below the hill a tractor ground backwards and forwards between the hedges. There was no other sound at all. Finally Hurst said, 'I didn't know —' but Merrow took him up at once.

'You didn't know you were acting queer? Of course you didn't. No one ever does, or they wouldn't do it. But your mind's in a mess, and it shows. You don't want people to think that, do you?'

Hurst looked up at him then, silent, but fighting against an enormous urge to talk, because this was a man he could talk to, perhaps the only person he could talk to. He said, 'John —' but once more Merrow cut off whatever it was he was going to say.

'No,' said Merrow. It was almost a shout. 'No, Mr. Hurst, I don't want your explanation, whatever it is. There's no call for you to explain anything, to me or anyone. It's yourself you've got to talk to. It always is in the long run, or that's what I've found. And maybe at the end of it all there's less to explain than you think. You make up your own mind, and make it up so as you won't hurt yourself or anyone else. Whatever is done is done, and you've no right to drag anyone else in. You've got more to look forward to in your life than most of us, and it's time you were getting on with it, not hanging about here and making trouble for yourself and other people.'

He swung away and walked over to the window, and stood there looking out. His hands were behind his back, gripped tightly together, so that the strain showed in the set of his shoulders. Gradually, as Hurst watched him, the grip relaxed, and his arms swung to his sides. The powerful shoulders stooped almost dejectedly, and after a bit he turned slowly and came back across the room to where Hurst still sat in his chair. He said, 'There, I'm sorry, Mr. Hurst, and I hope I haven't hurt your feelings. But it's time somebody talked straight to you, and that's a fact. I don't know much about you, other than what I've seen here. Have you got a father living?'

Hurst shook his head. 'Not since I was a child,' he said.

'Ever been in a job, then? I mean – I know you've got your own work, that's when you're doing it, but I mean, working under anyone, doing what you're told and told when to do it?'

He shook his head again. He seemed as dejected now as Merrow. 'Not really, no,' he said.

'Well, there you are. You need somebody to run your life for you. I know one that would do it, if you'd let her and she was fool enough to take you on. But that's no business of mine. Only you're too much on your own. I know' – he waved a hand comprehensively round the cottage – 'I know you can manage for yourself, run the house and all that. It's yourself you can't run. Maybe you could once, I don't know, but not the way you are now. You've been broken up, that's the truth, and I know who did it for you. You need putting together again, and you can't manage it for yourself. I dare say you tried, but it hasn't worked, or you wouldn't have come back here at all. Isn't that right?' Hurst looked up at him. He was entirely submissive now.

'That's right John,' he said.

Merrow nodded. He thought for a moment. Then he said, 'Got anything to drink in the house?'

'Only whisky.'

'Well, that's all right. Ever drink it?'

'Not often. I don't like drinking on my own. I've tried it, of course, but it didn't work.'

'Could be. How much have you got, then?'

'A bottle, pretty well.'

'Good. How'd it be if I came up later and helped you drink it? A bottle should do between us.'

Suddenly Hurst smiled at him. 'I'd like that,' he said.

'Well, for pity's sake. So should I. All right, I'll come up later. The bottle and two glasses, and water if you want it. Now I'll be going.' He went to the front door and opened it. 'Don't do anything silly till I come,' he said.

Hurst smiled at him again. 'I won't, I promise,' he said. He felt light headed, as if he had been drinking already. Merrow threw up his head and made a faint snorting sound. Then he went out and shut the door behind him. Hurst got up and looked round him. It was still early in the afternoon. He went through into the kitchen and got the whisky bottle out of the cupboard. He put it on a tray and put two glasses with it. He filled a small jug with water and put that on the tray too. Then he carried the tray into the sitting-room and put it on the table. There was no need to do it yet, but he wanted to feel committed. He turned the key in the front door, which Merrow had unlocked, and then went and let himself out at the back.

He could still hear the tractor, but could not see it. He could see nobody at all, but he was conscious now of every movement he made, in case somebody, somewhere, could see him. He tried to remember how he had walked in the days of his freedom, but could not think of anything special about it. He could have made a start by going out of the front door and down the path by Mrs. Basset's cottage, instead of going out of the back and skirting the edge of the wood, but this never occurred to him. He went along the edge of the wood with his eyes mostly on the ground. Every now and then he lifted his head and looked round him, like a grazing deer, to make sure everything was as he had last seen it; but like the deer, it was mainly the ground he was interested in. It was in fact at ground level that the edge of the wood was most interesting. There were no trees big enough, at least near the edges, to kill the small growth under them, and the greenery grew in a tangled mass nearly

104

head high. There were paths in and out of the wood, some of them smooth and well trodden, but they were tunnels big enough only for the badgers and smaller fry that lived there. If there had been deer in this part of the country, instead of a single man acting like a deer, they would have been in the wood by now, and breeding there, and some of the paths would have been cleared to a height which an agile man could make his way through without crawling or breaking the branches. But there was not enough woodland in these parts to attract them, and the deer had not come there yet. There were only the polished tunnels low on the ground, and the faint tracks on the grass that fanned out from them, growing fainter as they spread out and went away down the slope towards the water or whatever it was that the wood's inhabitants came out to look for. He could have taken a bill-hook, or even a strong stick, and forced his way into the wood at any point if he had wanted to, but he did not want to go into the wood at all. He went on along the edge of it, looking at the tunnel-mouths and every now and then lifting his head to look at the country round, and trying to think how he ought to behave in case anyone could see him. When he came to the farther end, he struck out and walked in a long circle through the fields, away from the direction in which he could still hear the tractor working. He saw nobody all the way.

It was past teatime when he got back, but he made himself tea and ate biscuits with it. He was not sure when Merrow would come, but he knew he would come with a substantial meal inside him. He himself did not feel up to a substantial meal at that time of day, but he needed something in his stomach, and in any case he could not see himself doing much cooking later. When he had finished, he put the things away and went into the sitting-room. The bottle still sat on the table. It was full to the bottom of the neck and made of plain glass, so that the whisky looked wonderfully rich against the yellow southern light from the windows. He loved whisky and liked being suitably drunk, but only in company. By himself, he resented the loss of control, and not knowing what he would do frightened him. He had tried getting drunk by himself, as he had told Merrow he had, but not again after the first few experiments. Getting drunk in casual company was no good either, because it offended his sense of privacy. He needed company he could trust, and that was rare. He looked at the whisky in the bottle with a curious respectful anticipation, as if it was a powerful and beneficient machine which he could not start for himself. He longed to see what it could do, but needed the expert to set it going.

Merrow came before he really expected him, but he had remembered to unlock the front door. There was the single solid rap of a hard knuckle on the panel, and then the door opened and Merrow came in. He gave Hurst a knowing, almost conspiratorial smile, as if they were all boys together, who had got away and were out on the spree. In the inside of his mind Hurst knew that it was all part of the act, like the smiling confidence the surgeon lavishes on his still un-anaesthetised patient, but he was glad of it all the same. Neither of them said anything, because they did not want to talk until they had the whisky inside them, but when Hurst had poured out two stiff ones and handed Merrow his glass, Merrow waved it and said, 'Happy days,' and for a moment Hurst wondered whether happy days might not after all be possible. They drank, and Merrow looked at what was left in his glass, which was not much. He said, 'Ah, I needed that. I've been working. You eaten?' and Hurst nodded.

The whisky flowered splendidly in his stomach. He said, 'I haven't been working, but I needed it too,' and Merrow laughed as if he had really said something amusing. They drank what they had left, and Hurst poured out two more, and this time it was he who said, 'Happy days,' and Merrow said 'That's right,' as if he had happiness in his personal power to bestow and meant by hook or by crook to bestow it. The light in the sky turned from yellow to white, and from white to fading blue. The room got almost dark, and Hurst would not have minded turning on the lights, but had no real wish to do so. Merrow sat where he was in his chair, and Hurst came and went between the table and the chairs with the bottle in his hand and the preternatural accuracy of the introvert drunk.

Merrow did nearly all the talking, all about the local people and nearly all of it bawdy. There was no innuendo and never a calculated punch-line, but the people he talked about were real people, not the stylised characters of the smoke-room joke, and the outrageous things they did and suffered had really happened. It was a world which had simmered all these years round Hurst's hill-top cottage, and which he had not so much cut himself off from as simply not assumed to exist. It was the world of Amy Basset and her lodger, and Lizz, for all her office manners, had her roots in it and knew where they were. He lapped himself in its rank vitality, and somewhere inside his swollen mind he remembered a dark church and another man, equally real at the time, talking about the grace and mercy of God. In the capacious clarity of alcohol he did not find the two incompatible, but he could not quite bring them together, though he felt he ought to be able to because both men had said the same. He got up and poured the last of the whisky into Merrow's glass. He hardly felt the bottle between his fingers, but did not spill a drop.

It was only when Merrow got up to go that he said anything about Hurst himself. He went to the door, moving rather ponderously, but perfectly steady on his feet. He groped for the door-handle, and his hand found the light-switch at the side of the door. He snapped it down and turned, and the two men stood blinking and smiling at each other in the unexpected light.

Merrow said, 'I don't know, I'm sure. There's nothing wrong with you, you know. I wondered, but there isn't. You're all right.'

Hurst was indignant now. He had thought he was over all that and did not want to go back to it. The light in his eyes made him feel top-heavy, and he stood with one hand on the back of a chair and his feet firmly planted, swaying so slightly that he was hardly conscious of the movement except at the extremity of each swing. His speech was perfectly clear. He said, 'Of course I'm all right. I may act queer, but —'

Merrow laughed, helplessly but benignly, as he had been laughing all the evening at the predicaments of his neighbours. He said, 'You do, by God, I told you, but it's not you. It's – I don't know, some sort of an act you're putting on, but you've got so as you can't help yourself. Well, you've got to help yourself.' He turned and opened the door to go out, but on the threshold he turned and spoke again. He said, 'There's nothing to worry about. I'm telling you. It's not there, it's gone and finished. You forget it and clear out. There's nothing to keep you.' He went a few steps out of the door, and as he went Hurst went a few steps up to the door, holding on to the doorpost with the hand that had been holding the chair. Then Merrow stopped and turned again. He said, 'You go to bed now and sleep it off. Drink all the water you can get down, and then you can piss the whisky out of you in the morning and think about it. You'll see I'm right.' He turned for the last time and went off down the path.

Hurst shut the door but did not lock it. He put the empty

glasses back on the tray with the empty bottle and
the still not empty jug, and carried them through into the
kitchen with the same iron concentration. He threw the
bottle into the bin. He emptied the jug into the sink and
swilled out the glasses and put them on the draining board
with the jug. Then he remembered Merrow's instructions
and filled one of the glasses with water and drank it off. He
drank several glasses. His stomach felt comfortably full, but
he did not feel at all sick. He turned out the lights and went
very slowly upstairs. He took off his clothes and washed his
face and hands, taking care not to bump his head on the
taps of the wash-basin. He went through the automatic
ritual of cleaning his teeth and emptying his bladder. He
stood for a moment, wondering if there was anything else
he ought to do, but he could not think of anything. A
heavy, triumphant satisfaction welled up in him, and he
walked through to the bedroom and dropped into the bed.

He slept at once and must have slept a long time. He
woke to full sunlight and a bursting bladder. He got up and
found himself light-headed but steady. He put on his dressing-gown and went through into the bathroom. The window was open but he did not look out, being busy with his
immediate need. It was only through the noise of the re-
charging cistern that he heard a car coming up the drive.

XII

He did not know who it was, but he did not want to be caught like this, because it made him feel guilty. He ran across to his room and scrambled into some clothes. Now that his bladder was empty, he was aware that his stomach was, too, and he felt more light-headed than ever. He had not brushed his hair or shaved, and he wondered what colour his face was, but he went downstairs rather than be found still up in his bedroom. He had forgotten, because it was so unusual, that he had slept with the doors unlocked. The back door opened as he came down the stairs and Christabel came in. She was perfectly turned out, as usual, and her eyes were angry. She said, 'What have you been saying to Charles?'

He frowned at her, and the muscles of his forehead hurt very slightly as they contracted. He said, 'Charles? When?'

'I don't know when, but I know you have been talking to him, and he's worried. What have you been saying?'

He put a hand up and smoothed back his tousled hair. He said, 'Would you like some coffee? I should.'

She said, 'No. Oh, yes, all right, if you want it. Haven't you had breakfast?' He shook his head. She looked him up and down. 'What have you been doing, drinking?' He nodded. 'I didn't think you did.'

He said, 'I don't usually. I had company.'

'Oh. Well, all right, but be quick. I mustn't stay long, and I've got to talk to you.'

He nodded again. He was beginning to be a little indignant himself. He said, 'Go on in and sit down. I won't be long.'

She had not sat down when he carried the tray in. She was standing in the window, as she had stood before, gazing down the slope towards Mrs. Basset's cottage. She did not say anything. He poured out two cups and carried one to the visitor's chair. 'Come and sit down,' he said. She took the cup and sat down, still looking at him, as tense as a coiled spring. He sat down opposite her, looked at her for a moment, and then drank his coffee. He felt enormously and instantaneously better. He said, 'Did Charles tell you I had spoken to him?'

'Not directly, but he implied it. When was this?'

'I see. A few evenings ago.'

'But you didn't tell me yesterday.'

'No, I didn't. There was no reason why I should. Will you have some more coffee?'

'No, go on, drink it yourself, for heaven's sake. You're no good to me in this state.'

He poured himself out a second cup and drank it. She watched him in silence and then put her own cup down on the table beside her. He did not think she had drunk much of it. Suddenly she said, 'Mike, what's going on?' The anger had all gone out of her and she seemed desperate. 'What is there between you and Charles that I'm not supposed to know about? I wouldn't mind that, only I know it's worrying him, and I can't bear it. Mike, what is it?'

He put his cup down too. He was at ease with his body again, and was moved by her distress. She was vulnerable, after all, much more vulnerable than Lizz would ever be. Lizz herself had said so. Take away her power of physical attraction, and she had few weapons left. She had not dominated him before. He had put himself in subjection to her. He said, 'Look, Christabel. I didn't talk to Charles be-

111

cause he was your husband. All right, yes, I did go to see him. I rang up and made an appointment. But what we talked about didn't concern you. Your name wasn't even mentioned. Charles didn't tell you about it either, did he? Or not at the time. If it had concerned you, I think he would have, don't you?'

She looked at him as if she was trying to believe him. He had said she could trust him before, and she had believed him. Now she was not so sure. She said, 'Why is he worried, then?'

He was worried himself now. He stared at the floor frowning, and this time his frown did not hurt him. He said, 'I don't know. I can't understand it. What makes you think he is?'

'Because he said so. He isn't a worrier, you know. He's too decisive. He takes things very seriously, but he doesn't worry about them. I think he has enough faith not to. But yesterday morning he was worried. I don't mean that he was distraught, but he did have something on his mind, and that's so unusual that it showed, and I asked him what is was. He hesitated a bit, but then he said it was you, or perhaps something that had happened between you and him, I don't know. I didn't ask him any more, I couldn't, and he didn't tell me. But of course I was upset. I was frightened, Mike. Can't you see that? I had to ask you.'

He said, 'Yes, I see,' but he saw very little. 'Look, Christabel,' he said, 'there are two things here. One I won't tell you and one I can't. I won't tell you what I saw Charles about, because that was between him and me. I went to him, if you like, as a priest, although that's not quite true, because I can't call myself a Christian. At any rate, I went to him for help and advice because he is a man whose judgement I'd respect. I don't know how you manage as a parson's wife, but my impression is that you leave that side

112

of his life to him.'

'Of course. I didn't marry him as a parson, I married him as a man. I love him as a man. He knows that. We had it all out, of course. You can't separate Charles the man from Charles the parson. He'd be a rotten parson if you could, and he's not that. But I leave his job to him, just as I should if he'd been a doctor or a bank manager or something. I'd have married him whatever he was. He couldn't have been a politician or a car-salesman, because then he wouldn't have been Charles, and then I shouldn't have married him.'

'All right, that's fine. Then will you take it that my meeting with him was part of his job, which you say you leave to him? What I can't tell you, because I don't know, is why it should be worrying him, if it really is. It wasn't – I don't know, I don't think in fact it was a very successful meeting. I felt something had gone wrong with it, and I thought perhaps he felt the same. But I don't think that was his fault, it was mine, because I couldn't really get the record straight. But so far as he could he gave me his advice, and I don't see him as a man troubled with second thoughts. You say yourself he isn't.'

She thought for a bit. She still did not look happy. Then she said, 'You say my name wasn't mentioned. I accept that. I agree, I think if it had been, if the discussion had been directly about me, Charles would have told me. But it's possible for two people to talk about another person without actually mentioning them, or even referring to them directly at all. At least, it is with women. I did it myself the other day. Are you sure it wasn't like that?'

He said, 'You and Lizz?'

'I'd forgotten you call her Lizz. Elizabeth Basset, yes. Did she tell you?'

'She told me she'd had a talk with you. She also said my name hadn't been mentioned.'

'Quite right, nor it had. But it was you we talked about, all the same. What did she say, Mike?'

'She said you'd wanted to have a look at her – vet her, was the way she put it – and that in fact you'd had a look at each other. She said she'd known you by sight for a very long time but never spoken to you.'

'I see. Well, that's fair enough. I trust she gave you a favourable report.'

Hurst was losing patience again. He said, 'Oh, come off it, Christabel. She was perfectly entitled to tell me if she wanted to, and you might have known she would. As a matter of fact, she liked you very much. She hadn't expected to, but she did. And you needn't be disparaging about it. I don't think she'd like anybody easily or without good reason.'

She smiled at him, quite suddenly, but it was a gentle smile. She said, 'All right, Mike. I didn't mean to offend. I didn't want to, really. I liked her, too. She's very intelligent and very determined.'

He was still not quite mollified, 'And very attractive,' he said.

'Then why in God's name don't you marry her? She's very much in love with you. You must know that as well as I do. You're not a complete innocent. When you were here before, she was the kid sister. She was probably quite happy just thinking you were marvellous. Now I expect she looks at you with a much more critical eye, but she wants you all the same, more than ever. Why not have her? She'd do you all the good in the world.'

He groped in his mind for an answer he could give her but could not find one. Instead he said, 'You didn't come here to tell me to marry Lizz, did you? We've got ourselves a bit side-tracked, haven't we?'

She took a breath to speak, but let it go in a small, audible sigh. Then she said, 'All right. Let's go back to what we were talking about, your meeting with Charles. I'm not asking you what you talked about, and I accept the fact that my name wasn't mentioned. But wasn't I to some extent in the back of your mind – in the back of both your minds, if it comes to that? Wasn't I to some extent involved, even if I wasn't mentioned?'

He thought about this. He was very serious now. After a bit he said, 'In a way, yes, though not directly. In my mind, I mean. I've no reason to think you were in Charles's.'

She looked at him equally seriously. She said, 'Aren't you underestimating him a bit? He's good with people, you know. It's his job, after all. He doesn't miss much.'

'I see. It hadn't occurred to me, I must say. You're afraid it may be that that's worrying him?'

She nodded. 'I don't pretend I'm being unselfish in this. I don't like Charles being worried, of course, I mean about anything. But I certainly don't want him worried about me. You're so damned self-centred, Mike. I don't think you can help yourself. You haven't got enough to think about, especially when you're not working. I think you might be inclined to air your own troubles, to Charles or anyone else, without stopping to consider the possible implications for other people.'

He did not look at her now. He sat staring unhappily at the floor between them, and she sat looking at him and waiting. Presently he said, 'I don't think I air my troubles, exactly,' and she made a small impatient sound in her throat.

'You don't exactly try to conceal them, do you? I know you don't tell anybody straight what it is that's troubling you, because it's not in you to do it. You hug it, the way some people hug their cancers. But you don't leave anybody in much doubt that the trouble's there. You come back here looking miserable, and you go about looking miserable, and

115

you don't seem to be able to do anything about it, even now you're here. I don't know what you have actually said, to Charles or anyone else. Very likely not much. But going on the way you do, the less you say, the more you leave to the imagination.'

He thought, going on the way I do, acting queer. The temporary relief he had gained from John Merrow had died out of him, and he felt abject again, abject and almost panic-stricken. There was a sudden shortening of time in front of him. It was no longer only a matter of making up his mind. Action, a decision of some sort, was being forced on him, not now by internal pressures, but by other people. He wanted Christabel to go away. He wanted everybody to go away and keep away and leave him to decide for himself. The fact that he had had five years and decided nothing did not occur to him as relevant. This was a new situation, brought on by his coming back here, and he must be left to deal with it himself. He had come back, in fact, to make a decision, but he had not expected the place to take over in this way. He had not known what it was he had expected here, but it was not that. He knew that he ought not to have spoken to Charles Richards now, and felt guilty because he had. But he had needed it desperately at the time, and it had seemed a harmless thing to do. Now he had Christabel sitting there looking accusingly at him, and he was filled with doubt about what he had really done. All the same, he had to say something, or she would never go. He said, 'Christabel, I can't answer for Charles's state of mind, and I certainly can't explain it. But I can assure you that I would not willingly have done anything to harm you, and I still don't believe I have. I said you could trust me, and I meant it. So far as I am concerned, you still can.'

They were looking at each other again now, both agitated, each obsessed with their own private trouble and not to any extent considering, or even fully believing in, the other's. She shook her head, slowly and sadly. 'I trust your good intentions, Mike,' she said. 'You're no Jack Basset, I know that. What I don't trust is your actual performance. I wish I could, but I don't think you're really in command of yourself.' She got up, also slowly, as if she could neither make up her mind to go nor see any purpose in staying. 'It's difficult for me to judge,' she said, 'because I don't know what it is that has got you into this position. From what you say, I suspect Charles is in the same difficulty as I am. I trust Charles in every respect. But I'm pretty desperately unhappy about him, all the same. Now I'd better be going.'

Hurst was on his feet too now. She moved past him without looking at him and went through the kitchen to the back door. He went after her, but she opened the door for herself. She said, 'Good-bye, Mike,' still without looking at him, and he said, 'Good-bye, Christabel,' and let her go, shutting the door after her. He heard her car start and turn and go off down the drive. He waited till he could no longer hear it. Then he turned and went back into the sitting-room. He gathered up the coffee things and took them to the sink, but did not wash them up. Instead he went upstairs to wash himself and shave and get properly dressed. He could not do anything else until he had done that. While he was doing it, he was trying to think what he would do when he was dressed. He did not get very far with it. The position was what it had always been. He had to do something, but did not know what to do. The only difference now was that he had to do something at once, and he was not only distressed but frightened. He was like the suicide whom a long process of indecision has brought almost unaware on to the parapet of the bridge and who suddenly sees how far there is to fall before he hits the water.

He went through the physical processes mechanically and

correctly. He was not a smart dresser, but he kept himself clean and as far as possible tidy, just as he did his undistinguished house and furniture, and by the same routine mechanisms. He would have shaved and brushed his hair before going to the gallows, not because he was concerned for his appearance on the scaffold, but because it was the proper thing to do and he would not feel right if he had not done it. He was aware all the time that the day was getting darker instead of lighter. The sky was heavily overcast, and the wind was getting up. The birds no longer sang in the wood, and he could hear the tops of the trees chafing uneasily among themselves. He shut the windows before he went downstairs, and downstairs it was darker than ever. He was weighed down with an intolerable oppression and lassitude, as if something outside himself, that he could neither cope with nor escape from, was closing in on him.

Escape, after a little, became the uppermost thought in his mind. He did not really believe in any freedom he could escape to, but at least he could get away from this place and these people. The place and the people were too much interested in him and knew too much about him. Whatever he had to do, he must do it alone, and here he did not feel alone any more. He stood for a time in front of the sitting-room windows, looking out at the dark country and the gathering storm. Then he went through into the kitchen. The coffee things caught his eye, and he washed them and put them away, because he could not go away and leave them as they were. He did it all with a sort of anguished efficiency, but in between he looked out through the window at the huddled, uneasy wood. Then, moving very slowly, he went upstairs and pulled his suitcases out from under the bed.

XIII

It was a cruel thing, a storm at this time of the year. The young leaves were heavy with the sap inside them and the rain outside, and still tight on their stems. When the gusts caught them, they tore whole branches of the soft wood away. The stuff that littered the ground was not the expend-able richness of autumn, but doomed fragments of the living tree. It could cling to a desperate life of its own until the rain stopped and the sun came out, and then it would wither and go into the ground, a good five months too early. The trees would mend again, of course, and the birds would patch their broken nests, or build new ones and lay fresh eggs if the whole lot had gone, but it was a cruel set-back, all the same. Hurst went gingerly, hating to step on what was underfoot and picking off the single leaves that settled and stuck on his wet raincoat. He went head down, trying to keep the rain out of his neck, but glad of the enormous disturbance round him because it suited his mood and gave him something to cope with, and that was what he had come out for.

He came to the bottom of his own hill, crossed the stream by a farm bridge of railway sleepers laid sideways on heavy joists, and set himself to climb the long slope opposite. He went steadily, concentrating on the wet ground underfoot and the wet air that battered him and blew his clothes about. He walked and scrambled, always upwards, for twenty minutes or more, and never paused or looked back. The barn was on the skyline ahead of him, half hidden in distracted trees. It was only in winter that it showed a clear hard outline, with the skeleton branches no more than a linear decoration. At this time of the year the trees just about let you see it was there, especially when they themselves were moving. By midsummer they all but hid it completely. The barn was of old stone roofed with tiles and open at one end. Whatever it had been built for, it was used now only for farm machinery and chemicals and fencing oddments, and when the sun got on it, it had a sour artificial smell. It was a sad place, stuck up there on the ridge by itself, but he liked it because he liked man-made walls better than a natural hill-top. It made somewhere to walk to, and there was never anyone there. At least it would keep the rain off. It was all right walking in the rain if you had a mind to it, but you could not stand still and think coherently in weather like this without something over your head.

He climbed over the last gate because it was wired up. If a gate had a fastening that worked, he would open it and walk through and fasten it after him, but if a farmer tied his gates, he must expect people to climb over them. He turned, almost at a run, into the open end of the barn and stood and straightened himself up in the dry silence. Both the dryness and the silence were only relative. The things in the barn shone with wet in places where the rain dripped through the roof, and the wind growled savagely round the stiff old building, but it was comfort compared with the world outside. He took his cap off and shook the loose water out of it, and undid the soaking collar of his coat from round his neck. Now that he was out of the wind, he found himself warm all through from his uphill walk. He mopped the rain off his face with his handkerchief, and felt the skin go moist again with a mild sweat. An elementary peace enveloped him, but he knew it would not stand up to much scrutiny or last if he stayed too long. He propped himself against the raised end of a tilted trailer, and wondered whether he would really, when he got home, put his bags in the car and drive off, and if so, where he would drive to. He told himself that even if he went, it would not be for long, let alone for good. He must come back here, as he had come now, because this was where the thing was and where the answer must be, if there was an answer. All the people who kept on telling him to go away could not understand that. But he might go for a day or two, perhaps, to escape from this immediate intolerable pressure which the people were building up round him.

He did not hear anything because of the noise the wind and rain made, but suddenly he saw a figure running, first shining and grey in the grey light outside, and then dark against it as it ran into the open end of the barn. It ran up to him, crouching as he had crouched, and then like him straightening up and flinging the wet covering back off its head. She panted as she faced him, her face flushed, her eyes wide in the gloom, her dark hair lank with the wet. She took hold of him by the front of his open coat, almost shaking him. She said 'Oh, Mike. Mike, are you all right?'

He took her hands in his, wet hands but warm under the wet skin. 'Lizz,' he said, 'what are you doing here? Why aren't you working?'

'I took the afternoon off,' she said. 'I wanted to see you. I came up to the cottage, and then I saw you coming up the hill, and I ran after you. I called out, but you couldn't hear, of course. You are all right? What did you come up here for?'

He let her hands go gently, and she stood there, still out of breath, peering up at him in the gloom. 'I often come up here,' he said.

'Do you? I didn't know. It's a bad place, Mike, you mustn't.' She looked up at the massive timbers of the roof. She was not really whispering, but her voice sounded very small in the huge disturbance round them. She said, 'A man hanged himself here. Did you know that? Before you first came, but I can just remember it. No one comes here, except the farm people when they have to.'

'That's why I like it, I suppose. I didn't know about the hanging. I didn't come here to hang myself, Lizz. I couldn't hang myself, wherever I was.'

'No, but – I don't know, Mike. I don't know what you'd do to yourself, sometimes. Not the way you are now. You wouldn't do that, Mike? Promise you wouldn't do that.'

'I wouldn't,' he said. 'I have already promised, in fact.' She frowned, and he said, 'Never mind who. Not Christabel, anyway. But it was an easy promise to make. I should never have the courage to do it.'

She shook her head at him. She said, 'You don't lack courage. If you did, you wouldn't have come back here at all. That's just part of your determination to under-value yourself. I don't know why you do it. I think it's some sort of let-out for yourself. You know? Who am I to deal with this? – that sort of thing. It's quite new. You used to be full of bounce. Anyway, it isn't courage you lack. You'd have the guts to do whatever you decided. The trouble is you can't decide.'

He did not say anything. He was conscious again of that enormous, irrelevant physical attraction, and he wanted to be warm and comforted more than he could ever remember wanting anything. But the attraction was irrelevant and the comfort was denied him, because there was no answer that way. She said, 'I know the answer, Mike. I don't know the question, but I know the answer. You must surrender. I don't mean run away, I mean surrender positively. It takes courage to surrender, because it's a sort of self-sacrifice. Can't you see that?'

He roused himself at last. He was still groping, but somewhere in the back of his mind there was a glimmer of hope. 'Surrender to whom?' he said.

She smiled at him. It was the sort of smile the patient grown-up gives at the child's woeful inability to understand. She said, 'Me, of course. You don't need anyone else. I can't think why you can't see that. It seems so obvious to me.'

She held out her hands to him, and he took them, but he was still at a loss. He said, 'But what would you do with me, Lizz, if I did surrender to you?'

She was no longer smiling. She was perfectly serious and matter-of-fact. She said, 'Love you, of course. What else is there to do with you?'

He thought about this, because that was what she wanted him to do. He said, 'I see,' but he did not see, not yet. 'But wouldn't that be your sacrifice, not mine?'

'No, no, no, no.' She shook his hands impatiently, almost with exasperation. 'I should have what I wanted, shouldn't I? What sacrifice is there in that? In any case, it doesn't matter who makes the sacrifice, so long as it's made. It's only your egotism that won't let you see that. Why do you want to hog the action so? You're not very good at it, not at the moment, are you?'

Her hands were cold in his now, and she shivered suddenly. He said, 'You've got wet, haven't you? I mean, really wet, through your coat?'

She nodded. 'I didn't come dressed for this, that's the truth. I was going up to the cottage, not all this way. But it doesn't matter. I'll get warm going back.'

But her physical distress worried him and would not let him think. He said, 'Let's go back, then, Lizz. I can't talk to you when you're cold and I'm warm. And if you're wet through, you'll only get colder, the longer you stay. Let's go back now before you get really cold. Then you can go and

put on some dry clothes, and we'll go on talking. All right?'
She took her hands out of his. She seemed utterly dejected.

'All right,' she said, 'if that's what you want.' She began
to do up her flimsy defences against the weather. He could
see now how flimsy they were. 'But Mike,' she said, 'will
you try to understand what I've been saying? Please do try
to understand. It's the only hope for either of us.'

He said very seriously, 'I think I do understand. And it's
something I hadn't thought of before, not quite like that.
But I can't see my way through it yet. I must think about it.
But I can't think here, not with you in this state.' He buttoned his own coat round him and put his cap on. It bound
his head tightly in a band of cold dampness, and he too
shivered. 'Come on,' he said. 'We'll go together and take it
steady. But we must go.'

He held out a hand, and she took it, and they went out of
the dark barn into the brighter chaos outside. The wind was
on them at once, and it was raining as hard as ever, but all
they had to do now was to keep moving, and in less than
half an hour they would be home. It did not matter how
wet they got so long as they kept moving, and the wind was
behind them now, driving them down the slope. They let
go of each other's hand only when there were gates to climb
or the path was too narrow for them to walk side by side.
They did not laugh at their physical predicament, as a pair
of lovers might have done, or let it worry them as if it had
any power over them. They ignored it as irrelevant. Very
nearly they ignored each other, so deep were they in their
own thoughts. They held hands because each was relevant
to the other and their problem was a common one, even if
they thought about it differently and separately. There was
not much physical comfort in it, any more than there was
discomfort in the weather.

They came to the bottom at last and crossed the bridge,

and when they came to the end of the wood, they let go of each other for the last time and Lizz went ahead along the narrow path under the edge of the tortured, lashing trees. Hurst walked as he nearly always walked with his eyes on the ground, and did not see until they were almost at the back of the cottage that John Merrow was standing there waiting for them. Lizz saw him and ran up to him, and he put out an arm and pulled her to his side, so that when Hurst looked up, they were standing there side by side, watching him as he came up. He saw the two faces together, and knew at once, and wondered why he had never seen it before. Lizz was no Basset, she was John's child. At most she was Jack's half-sister, in so far as Jack had had any of his mother's blood in him. He remembered her saying her mother had always been sweet on John. Perhaps the long dead Basset had had some excuse for his tyranny after all, or more likely he had brought it on himself. He looked from one face to the other, and Lizz looked at him as if she did not know at all what he had in his mind, and Merrow looked at him with a small, challenging smile, as if he knew very well.

He said, 'You're soaked, the pair of you. It's fool weather to go walking in. I don't know.' He was large and friendly and well wrapped up, and the weather made no more impression on him than it did on the back wall of the cottage.

Hurst said, 'I'm all right. I'm dressed for it. It's Lizz is the wet one.'

Merrow looked down at her. 'That's right,' he said. 'You run on down and get some dry things on before you get chilled.'

He took his arm from her, and she stood looking from one to the other of the two men, as if she could not make up her mind to leave them together. Hurst said, 'Go on, Lizz. John's quite right. It won't help anybody if you get pneu-

125

monia.' It was inarguably sensible, but he wanted her to go in any case, and she knew it.

It was John she was looking at now. He smiled at her but did not say anything. He was a man who never said anything twice. She said, 'All right.' She looked back at Hurst. 'You'll get changed, too?' she said.

'I will, I promise, as far as I need.'

She nodded and went off round the end of the cottage, a bedraggled figure, but resolute and quick moving as ever once she had made her mind up. The men watched her go and then turned to each other. Hurst said, 'Better come in, John,' and Merrow nodded, and the two of them went in through the back door into the kitchen.

They took off their caps and raincoats, shaking water everywhere on the tiled floor. Hurst climbed out of his boots, but found his trousers wet at the knee and his jersey at the neck. He stood there, undecided, looking at Merrow. He had shoes to put on, but his clothes were all in his suitcases upstairs. Merrow said, 'Better change those things, or you'll get cold. And she's sure to ask me.' He smiled, as at a small joke inside the family.

Hurst said, 'All right, only —'

'You're all packed up? I know. I saw the cases when I came in looking for you. You'll have to unpack a bit. You can't even travel in wet clothes. That's if you're travelling.'

'All right. I won't be a moment. Don't go.'

'Don't worry. I won't. You get any more whisky in?'

'Afraid not. I haven't been out. I mean, only just now, for a walk.'

Merrow nodded. He went over to where his dripping raincoat hung on the door and put his hand into an inside pocket. It came out with a flat quarter-bottle in it. 'That's what I thought,' he said. 'I'll put the kettle on. Got any lemon, then?'

Hurst said, 'In the fridge.' He felt relieved that he had not been found completely wanting.

'That's right. You go up and change, then.' He turned with the kettle to the tap over the sink, and Hurst went upstairs.

The room looked already like a hotel bedroom after breakfast, when the staff have been in and tidied, and only the packed cases show that it is still technically occupied. The air felt shut in. It was almost dark, and the rain lashed the outside of the windows. He did not want to go out in it again, even as far as the car. He was glad of the big man downstairs who stood between him and his escape. Lizz's father. Something in his pattern of things had shifted significantly, but he had not had time yet to work out its significance. He opened the case he wanted and pulled out a spare sweater and trousers. Merrow put the kettle back on the side table as he came downstairs and the sweet fumes came off the glasses to meet him. He said, 'Thank you, John,' and they took their glasses and went through into the sitting-room. It was wickedly dark for the time of day, but they had no need of lights.

They waved their glasses at each other and sipped, but this time there were no incantations for happiness. After a bit Merrow said, 'Look, Mike – do you mind if I call you Mike?'

'I'd like it very much.'

'Good. Well, look. There's nothing wrong with you. I told you. You've got yourself in a spot, but you're not the first. But I know you better now, and I tell you, there's nothing wrong with you. If there was, I'd see you dead first. You know what I mean?'

Hurst nodded. They were both immensely serious. 'I know,' he said. 'I've only just seen. Does Lizz know?'

'She feels it, you know? I don't think she's told herself

127

straight out. But that doesn't matter. You've been talking to her?'

'Yes. She followed me out, you know. I wouldn't have taken her out like that in this weather.'

'No, that's what I thought. She'd go after you wherever you were if she thought you needed it. You'd better make up your mind to that.'

Hurst nodded. 'I know.'

'Well, then —' The knock came, loud and emphatic, on the front door. Merrow said, 'Who the hell's that?'

Hurst put his glass down and went to the door and opened it. For a moment he did not recognise the big muffled figure. The wind swirled round them blowing the curtains about.

Charles Richards said, 'I want to talk to you. May I come in?'

XIV

Immediately Hurst was at a loss. He could not make his apprehension explicit, and he had no time to think about it. He merely felt the incompatibility of the two men, one behind him in the sitting-room and one in front of him on the doorstep, and the impossibility of keeping them apart. The fact that they were both men he liked and respected made it worse, not better. Practically, he had no choice. You could not keep a dog on the doorstep in this weather. He stood back and said, 'Of course. Come in.'

Richards had come by car, obviously. They would not have heard it with the racket there was outside. He had been in the rain only between the car and the door, and he was only superficially wet. He came straight in and Hurst shut the door behind him, forcing it against the wind. When he turned round, he saw that Merrow had got up, and the two men were facing each other in silence. He came round from behind Richards and stood between them. The ordinary civilities provided the necessary words for him to say, and there was nothing he could do anyway. He said, 'Do you two know each other? Charles, this is Mr. Merrow. John, Mr. Richards.' Richards had loosened his coat and his dog-collar was visible, but Merrow would probably know him by sight in any case. He doubted if Richards would have known Merrow by sight. Whether the name conveyed anything to him he did not know. It would depend on Christabel, probably. This was Christabel's country more than her husband's. He did not know how much she had told him about the people.

The two men shook hands and made the conventional noises, two big men exchanging powerful grips and sizing each other up. He had a momentary incongruous view of himself as a referee in the ring with a pair of heavyweights, but it would not do except in purely physical terms. He did not suppose that, even as their host, he had any control over either of them. They must work it out between them. Whatever Richards thought, he did not hesitate, but took his line at once. He turned to Hurst. He was immensely serious. There was an undercurrent of agitation in his voice and manner, but he was quite determined. He said, 'I thought I must talk to you. I've been thinking a lot about the matter we discussed the other evening. I didn't know you had company, of course.' He turned to Merrow. 'It's fairly urgent,' he said, 'and I'm afraid fairly private. I don't know – I wonder if you could excuse us? Or I could wait, if you have business to settle.'

There was no shadow of offence in it. He made no assertion of privilege, either professional or social. He rested his request on nothing but the need as he saw it, but he made it clear that he saw it as paramount. Merrow took him up on exactly similar terms. He smiled, looking from one to the other of them, gentle but quite immovable. He said, 'That's up to Mike, of course. It's his house. But I reckon myself a friend of his, and I reckon he needs friends. I know he's in a bit of a fix, and I've talked to him about it, too. I wonder if we couldn't discuss it together?'

There was no offence in this either, but it took Richards utterly by surprise. Despite Merrow's deferment to Hurst's wishes, neither of them looked at him. They were concerned only with each other. Christabel had said that Charles was good with people and did not miss much. Hurst wondered what he would make of Merrow. He did not think he could miss the obvious honesty and kindness in him. He thought he would probably also suspect a fundamentally different viewpoint, but this might not weigh with him. The question was whether Merrow's qualities were the only consideration. From what Christabel had said, and from Richards's barely concealed agitation, he did not think they were. Richards had not come to talk only about Hurst. He had come to talk, at least to some extent, about himself, and that put Merrow's presence in a very different light. Richards still had not spoken. He and Merrow were still looking at each other, almost as if Hurst was no longer there.

Finally Richards said, 'I wonder,' and Hurst made up his mind.

He said, 'Charles, John is a friend of mine, as he says. He is also a man whose judgement I very much respect, as I do yours. And I vouch for his discretion, absolutely. Of course I will talk to you alone, if you wish it. But I myself have no objection whatever to John's hearing whatever we have to say. Is that any good to you? It is I who am asking for help, after all.'

They spoke quite quietly, just loud enough to hear each other. The wind still tore at the roof and moaned in the chimney, and the rain threw itself intermittently against the windows. It was getting quite dark in the room now, but nobody thought of putting the lights on. Richards unbuttoned his coat slowly and threw it over a small chair by the door. Hurst thought it was the chair Lizz had put her cloak on, that first evening when she had come up the path under the silent rain. It seemed a very long time ago now. Everything had been completely quiet then, and he had been alone when she had come up. Now she was down in the cottage below, changing out of her soaked clothes, and these two men were here, both concerned with what he might do, and neither of them taking very much notice of him.

Richards said, 'All right. I agree it's for you to decide,' but Hurst knew that it was really he who had decided, and he had decided because he had made up his mind about John. They all sat down, Richards and Merrow in the two arm-chairs, and Hurst on a hard chair by the table. Richards said, 'I told you the other evening what I thought you ought to do. I don't think what I told you was right. Or perhaps really I don't think I said what I did for the right reasons, and that almost certainly vitiates the advice I gave you.'

Merrow said, 'What did you tell him?' and Richards stopped speaking to Hurst and spoke only to Merrow.

He said, 'I told him that whatever he did, he had to think of other people first. He had no right to settle his own diffi-culties at the possible expense of other people.'

Merrow nodded. 'What's wrong with that?' he said.

'Nothing in itself, perhaps. I don't know. The trouble is, I was one of the other people I was asking him to consider.' He thought for a moment. 'I or other people I was con-cerned with. It's the same thing. I don't think it was the advice I ought to have given him.'

Merrow said, 'What did you tell him to do, then?'

'I told him to go away. To go away from this place alto-gether and work out his own salvation somewhere else. That wasn't right, because I didn't really think he could do it. It is his salvation I ought to have been concerned with. I must be, as a priest, even if he does not see salvation quite as I see it. But I did not advise him as a priest. I advised him as a man, and as a man I was frightened.'

Merrow said, 'What you told him may have been right, all the same. It's what I've told him, more or less. I was thinking of myself, too – myself and other people. But I still think that what I told him was right.'

'No,' said Richards, 'no. I'm glad you have an interest to declare, too, because it makes it easier for me to appeal to your disinterested apprehension of what is right. We have no right, either of us, to ask Mike to carry his burden alone because we are afraid of what may happen if he tries to shed it. I don't know what his burden is. Perhaps you have a better idea than I have. I only suspect its nature and its implications, and my suspicions made me afraid. But it was utterly wrong of me to let my fear influence my judgement of his need.'

Merrow said nothing for a bit. He looked at Richards, smiling his small, quiet smile. He looked very much the more assured of the two. 'I wonder,' he said, 'whether there isn't a bit of selfishness in it either way. I mean, aren't you more worried about your own honesty than about Mike's salvation? If that's what you call it. I don't know much about salvation, myself. I want to get Mike out of the mess he's in, and if that's the same thing, fine. I'm much less worried about my own interests. I have them, of course. I want to buy his house, for a start. But that's not going to make me think that what I've told him is wrong.'

Richards leant forward in his chair, clasping his hands in front of him. He was less agitated now, but even more in earnest. 'Look,' he said, 'I am not going to argue about the nature of salvation. I do not expect you to see it as I see it, but I think you understand its nature as well as I do. What I am saying is that Mike is not going to be right with himself, or with other people, or as I believe with God, until he has told what is troubling him to whoever it is that has a right to know. As for myself, I have made you a present of my own shortcomings, and it is a long time since I did that with anybody except God. That is because I know Mike is right to trust and respect you. But like you, I am not going to let that influence my conviction of what is right. I have given him false guidance once, and I have paid heavily for it in my own conscience. I won't do it again.'

133

For a moment no one spoke, and then a gust hit the side of the cottage with a thud which they could feel as well as hear. The rain was less now and the cloud-wrack getting thinner. The last glimmer of daylight touched the three faces as they turned instinctively to the windows. Merrow said, 'Blowing itself out. We'll have a clear sky presently, and the wind will have gone by morning. Then we can see the damage. It's bound to be bad, coming at this time of the year.' He turned to Richards again. 'What I can't understand,' he said, 'is what good it's going to do Mike knowing he's hurt a lot of people. You may feel fine, suffering for conscience' sake and all that.' He stopped and shook his head. 'No,' he said, 'that's not fair. I don't think that of you. If you were involved – I say if, I'm not sure you could be, in fact – you'd suffer with the rest of us, I don't doubt, and not enjoy it any more than we would. But I still don't see how all that's going to help Mike. He's not a hard one. He's self-centred, it's true, but that's mostly being on his own. He does mind about other people. Otherwise he wouldn't be in the mess he's in.'

Richards said, 'He minds about himself, too – what I choose to call his own salvation. Otherwise he wouldn't be here at all. You can't judge everybody by yourself. You're different. You're secure in yourself, and you can afford to let other people come first. God knows, that's not a bad thing. Maybe you need God's help less than most of us. But Mike needs help. He's lost without it. And he won't get it until he has got rid of whatever it is standing in the way.' He turned to Hurst, still silent, crouched on his hard chair, slowly and ponderously, like an older and tireder man. 'I had better be going,' he said. 'I have done what I can.' He went over to the door and took up his coat from the chair. Then he turned again, looking at them both as he heaved his great shoulders into it and buttoned it closely round him. Neither of them had moved. He went to the door and put his hand on the handle. Then he turned again. 'God bless you both,' he said. He opened the door as little as he need, edged his way out into the wind and shut it heavily behind him. They both sat listening for the car, but once again they did not hear it.

It was Merrow who got up first. He heaved himself out of his chair with sudden unnecessary violence, as if he was breaking away from something that held him down. He moved across towards Hurst, and then changed his mind and went over to the door and switched on the light.

Hurst was on his feet now, too, but standing quite motionless. His face was ashy pale. Merrow looked at him. He looked immensely grave. He said, 'You never drank your drink after all.' His own glass was empty, though Hurst could not remember seeing him empty it.

Hurst picked up his glass from the table. He picked it up with exaggerated care, as he had when he was drunk. His hand was quite steady. He lifted the glass and sniffed at it. It smelt a little sickly now it was cold. 'No,' he said, 'I forgot about it. Sorry.'

'May as well drink it. It won't do you any harm, and it's a pity to waste good stuff.'

Hurst drank it obediently. He shivered slightly as the drink went down and put his glass back on the table so gently that it did not make a sound. He said, 'Thank you, John. Sorry I let it get cold.'

Merrow said, 'I must be going, too, that's the bugger of it. I can't stay out while it's blowing like this, or they'll be coming up when they see the lights.'

'Yes,' said Hurst, 'yes, you go along down.'

'You won't be travelling tonight?'

'Not tonight, no. It's a bit late now. I'll unpack what I need.'

'And you'll be here tomorrow?'

They looked at each other very fixedly, and Hurst nodded. 'I'll be here tomorrow, yes.'

'That's right. I'll see you're not disturbed.' He went through into the kitchen to find his coat, and Hurst gathered up the empty glasses and followed him. The hanging coats had left pools of water on the tiled floor, and Hurst got a mop out of the cupboard and mopped it up while Merrow put his coat on. 'I'll be off, then,' he said. 'Good night, Mike.'

Hurst said, 'Good night, John,' and Merrow went out of the back door as Richards had gone out of the front, edging out of it and shutting it quickly behind him.

Hurst rinsed the glasses and put them away. The wind had got him to itself now. It raged round the house, shutting him in more than ever and never letting him be. It left him no chance to think coherently, any more than it would have if he had been out walking in it, and now there were no other minds here to anchor his thought on. He was exhausted, mentally and physically, but could not rest. He was hungry, too, but though he recognised his need in a detached, clinical sort of way, he could not face the business of getting himself food and eating it. The wind increased his terrifying sense of urgency, but would not let him settle to any course of action. He left the light on in the kitchen, but went through and turned out the light in the sitting-room, where it could be seen from below. No one would come up the path, because Merrow had promised that they would not, but he did not want them even thinking about him. He clung to his desperate loneliness as the last refuge he had left.

He went upstairs to his room, but did not want the light on there either. He walked across to the window, avoiding the open suitcase on the floor with the same somnambulistic precision that governed all his movements. You could hear the wood up here. Downstairs you could only hear the wind, but up here you were level with the tops of the trees, and they wailed and fought like tethered and tormented beasts. He drew the curtains close, but there was no light to keep in, and they did nothing to keep out the sound. He pulled some blankets out from where he had put them away and threw them on the bed, but it was no good lying up here with the wood howling at him like that, and after a little he went downstairs again.

The wind blew most of the night, and the man went up and down between one dark room and the other, blinking as he passed through the lighted kitchen, and finding no peace anywhere. Charles had said he would find no peace, and his mind fastened on the words as the definition of his despair, feeling it more bitterly because it was thus fixed and focussed for him. Towards morning he lay down on the bed for the last time and pulled the blankets round him, conscious as he did so that the wind was falling now and the voice of the wood less full of menace.

He awoke to find daylight outside the curtains and total silence. For a moment he lay there, staring at the ceiling, and then he sat up and threw the blankets off him. He had sweated in his sleep, and the air struck cold at him through his clothes, but he did not wait to change them or put on any more. He got up off the bed and went downstairs. The kitchen light burnt yellow and useless in the daylight, and he walked over and turned it out. Then he took the key from the nail over the draining-board of the sink and went outside to the shed. He unlocked the door and opened it and left it open. He was moving steadily, but breathed through his open mouth, as if he was running. He went into the shed and picked up the spade from its place against the wall. He walked across to the wood with it, looking for a place he thought he remembered.

XV

It was very nearly the point of the wood nearest to the north-west corner of the cottage. Not quite, because the trees had grown close together at that particular point, even then, and he had had to go a little beyond them. Now the trees were the same, only taller and a little thicker, but it was the growth between them that had changed. It was a dense interlacing mass, head-high in places, and full of bramble and thorn. He swung his spade up, edge forward, and slashed furiously at the tangled green. The spade tore the branches apart, but was not sharp enough to cut them, so that all he had in front of him, for all his slashing, was a sort of elastic gap, which he could force his way through at the cost of his clothes and hands, but which all but closed behind him. There was not much storm debris in the wood itself. It had all blown clear of the wood to the eastward. There the whole slope of the hill was littered with it. Where he was, down between the trunks of the trees, there was only the dense mass of the wood itself, which the wind had hardly touched. He slashed and pushed his way into it, soon out of breath and sweating in good earnest, making his way in towards the centre of the wood.

He was conscious of his physical exhaustion now, in a way he had not been before, but there was nothing he could do about it except rest occasionally and wipe the sweat out of his eyes. When he rested, the silence round him was absolute. With him slashing about like this, the birds would not sing and the creatures that lived in the wood would not move. Even outside there was no wind at all, and here the air was trapped and motionless. His clothes were soaked through, with the sweat inside them and the wet greenery outside, but he felt no touch of chill. When he had got his breath back, he lifted the spade and went on again, hacking at the undergrowth in front of him. He hoped he was on the right line. No one could get lost in a wood of this size, but to follow a particular line and arrive at a particular point was not easy. There had been a clearing before, as far as he could judge right at the centre point of the wood. It had not been more than a few yards across, but it was unmistakable because no trees grew there, and there was a small stretch of clear sky overhead. It had had grass on it then. Now he supposed the undergrowth would have closed over it, but there would still be no trees, or nothing of any size. He would recognise it when he got there, so long as he did not miss it altogether, and hack his way clean out to the other side of the wood without finding it.

He did not know how often he had rested and gone on again. He was beginning to get a little desperate now, and his sense of time was distorted. As had happened so often before, he had taken a decision only to find that it did not work out as he expected. He felt himself struggling in an endlessly elastic net of unforeseen consequences. It was only after he had rested long enough, bent forward over the gripped handle of his spade, and raised his head to go on, that the thought suddenly came to him that he had reached the place he was looking for. He had not recognised it at first, because there were trees there, but now he saw that, to both sides of him and some way ahead, the trees were very small, barely higher than the encumbering undergrowth. He could not see more than a glimpse of sky, but the light was whiter and much stronger. For five years' growing, the trees were unexpectedly big, but they were still much smaller than in the rest of the wood. The size and shape of this island of young growth was about right, too. It must be his clearing, but it was not only the undergrowth which had filled it. It had filled up with trees, too, and they would have their roots everywhere. He went on a pace or two, and set about clearing the undergrowth altogether from a few square yards in the middle of what had once been the grassy clearing in the middle of the wood.

There were only two trees in the area he cleared, and these he did not touch. He got the smaller stuff away first, hacking and pulling at it, and then raking it aside until it was piled up like a rough fence round the place where he worked. Then he started to dig. His spade ran into roots at once, so that he could hardly even take a full spit the first time or lift a spadeful of earth clear in one piece. After only a few minutes he stopped again, leaning on his spade and trying to gather his wits to face up to the consequences of these unanticipated conditions. Except for his laboured breathing the wood fell silent again, and he heard, in the silence, something moving behind him.

He straightened up with a jerk and whipped round to face the direction the sounds were coming from. For a moment he held his breath and then, when he could hold it no longer, opened his mouth wide so that his breathing was as far as possible silent. The sounds went on. They were quite gentle, but so persistant that in that silence you could not think of them as furtive. Whatever was making the sounds knew it was making them and must know that they could be heard some way off. But whatever it was, it did not mind. The sounds went on, gentle but persistent, but getting nearer all the time. There was no denying now what the sounds meant. Someone or something was coming towards him, by the way he had come, forcing its way slowly and patiently through the passage he had partially cleared.

He whipped round again and began shovelling the earth he had lifted back into the small hole he had so far dug. He shovelled it in frantically, and levelled it down as far as he could, and spread the leaf mould over it until, at least to a very casual inspection, the ground did not look as if it had been disturbed. The sounds were very close now. He wondered if he could hide the spade, but this was nonsense with the hacked and uprooted undergrowth piled round him like that. Instead he turned and stood with the spade behind him, facing whatever it was that was coming slowly towards him through the wood. His mouth was still open and his eyes stared. His clothes clung to him and his hair was matted with sweat. He stood there, a living picture of desperation, and waited.

He could hear breathing now. It was human breathing, the breathing of steady and persistent human effort. Even with a passage partially cleared for them, whoever it was was finding it heavy going. There was visible movement now, and then, quite suddenly, two hands came up and put the branches aside and he saw Merrow looking at him between them. His face was seamed with worry, but when he saw Hurst, it changed and relaxed. He let his breath go in a long sigh. Then, quite slowly, he smiled and shook his head. 'Looking for something?' he said.

Hurst did not say anything. He stood there, staring at Merrow as if he was hypnotised. At last he nodded.

Merrow said, 'There's nothing there.' He came on the remaining yard or two, forcing his way through the undergrowth between them, and stepped into the small clearing Hurst had made. He looked at the ground for a moment and then back at Hurst. He said again, 'There's nothing there. It's no use, Mike. There's nothing there.'

For a moment more Hurst stared at him, totally at a loss, hung between his complete faith in the man and the com-

plete incomprehensibility of what he said. Then he turned
suddenly and leant his spade against one of the two young
trees behind him. He came back, wiping the sweat off his
face with his sleeve, and stood close in front of Merrow,
peering at him, trying to make him out. At last he shook his
head. 'I don't know what you mean, John. I know what I'm
looking for. I know it's there.'

Merrow said, 'I know what you're looking for, too. I
know it's not there. Can't you accept that? Can't you tell
yourself it's not there and never has been?'

Hurst shook his head again, and turned and went back to
his spade. 'No,' he said, 'no, look, I'll show you. Only the
suitcase. I wasn't going to —'

Merrow put a hand out and took the spade from him. He
let it go, unresisting. Merrow said, 'The suitcase isn't there,
either. All right, it was. So was he. But they're not there
now, neither of them, not for years now, not since just after
you left.'

For quite a long time the two men stood there looking at
each other, not moving and not saying anything. Somewhere in the wood a blackbird took advantage of the silence
and tried out a couple of preliminary trills. It stopped for a
moment and then, encouraged by the continued silence,
launched out into full morning song. Another blackbird,
unable to let this go unchallenged, answered the first from
its own territory. Other birds came in with an obligato of
lesser voices, and soon the whole wood was full of song.
When Hurst spoke, he spoke almost in a whisper, as if he
did not want to break in on it. He said, 'How did you
know?'

'I saw you bringing him back.' Merrow did not whisper,
but his voice came in a soft, deep rumble. 'I didn't know
about the suitcase. I found that here. It wasn't hardly covered. That was crazy, if you like.' He stopped and then

142

straightened himself, squaring his shoulders. The spade hung like a toy in his hands. 'Come on, Mike,' he said. 'You'd better tell me, and then I'll tell you. But not here. The sooner we're out of here, the better. You're wet through, for one thing, and I'm pretty wet myself. And I don't expect you've eaten anything since God knows when. We'll go back to the cottage and then you can tell me. Right?'

Hurst nodded, and Merrow turned and started back the way he had come. For a moment Hurst looked round at the small clearing as if he did not know what it was all about. Then he went after Merrow. He went close behind him, slipping through the openings the bigger man made. The passage was clearer now, and they did not make much noise between them. It was only close to them that the birds stopped singing. In all the rest of the wood they were still at it, full bat. When they came out at the side of the wood, Merrow made straight for the shed. He put the spade inside it and shut the door but did not lock it. They were neither of them a man to leave a spade uncleaned. Hurst watched him shut the shed and then followed him into the back door of the cottage.

He went upstairs and changed his wet clothes, and Merrow made tea in the kitchen. They took it into the sitting-room, and Merrow gave him a cup with a lot of milk and sugar in it, but this time nothing stronger. Hurst gulped it down, and Merrow got up and poured him out a second. All this time no one said anything. When he was back in his chair, Merrow said, 'All right, better tell me from the beginning. Then we'll know how we stand.'

Hurst started talking at once and, once he had started, did not pause or hesitate. He had been over it all in his head, over and over again, and it was all there, ready to be let go. He had never, all these years, thought it would be

Merrow he said it to, but it would have come out much the same, whoever it was. He said, 'I went round there that night to see her. I'd been trying to see her for weeks, but she'd been keeping me off. I was almost out of my mind about it. I used to go as soon as it was dark and hang about the house if I knew she was at home. If there was a light in her room, I used to go up to the window, in case the curtains weren't properly drawn and I could see if she was alone. But they always were, and I didn't dare tap on the window in case she had somebody with her. I used to spend hours there, until the lights went out, and then I knew she'd gone upstairs. She never opened the curtains, not at night. She just put the lights out, and then I knew she'd gone, and I took myself off. But I couldn't go till she had, just in case.

'Then that night for the first time one of the curtains wasn't properly drawn. There were the two windows, the ordinary window in front of the house and the french window round at the side. I couldn't see anything from the front, but when I went round to the side, I could. I suppose she'd opened it to let him in, and they hadn't put the curtains back carefully enough between them.

'I couldn't see much, but I could see enough. I could see both of them. I watched them for quite a long time. I couldn't help myself. I got a kick out of it, do you see? Do you know anything about jealousy? I tell you, I was physically excited, and all the time I was hating him with a sort of hatred I didn't know I had in me. I watched them until he got up, and then I realised he'd be coming out, and I was still standing there outside the window. I ran back across the grass and into the trees by the drive. I must have taken a different line from when I went in, because in the dark I fell over his suitcase. He must have put it down there before he went in, and I went headfirst over it, and knocked my head on a tree. I didn't knock myself out or anything, but I was pretty far gone anyway. I came down with my hand against a big stone. I got up on my knees and started bashing at the suitcase with it. As if it was him, I suppose. It was all I had to hit. Then I looked up, and he was coming across the grass, quite close to me. He must have heard me bashing at the case, but I didn't think of that. I stood up. I still had the stone in my hand, but I held it behind me.

'He came up to me, just inside the edge of the trees. It might have been all right then if he had kept his mouth shut. But he didn't. He said something about her. I won't tell you what he said, but feeling as I did, about him and about her, it finished me. He didn't know that, of course. He wasn't one to take much notice of other people anyway. I suppose he thought there wasn't anything to be afraid of, and he was angry about his case. He knelt down and started looking at what I'd done to it, and I hit him on the back of the head. I only hit him once, but it was a big stone, and I felt the bone go. He went flat down on his face, half across the case, and I stood there, watching him.

'Then he raised himself on his hands and knees. He didn't put a hand to his head or anything. He just stayed there on his hands and knees, crying. I tell you, he was crying like a little boy who's bumped his head in the dark. He said, "You silly bastard, what did you want to hit me like that for?" He couldn't understand, do you see, not even then. He couldn't see what he'd done to me, only what I'd done to him. He just crouched there, grizzling quietly, and then his arms gave way, and he went down on his face again. I dropped the stone and went to him, but I knew he was dead, even before I touched him. There didn't seem to be any blood. It was a round stone, you see. It had hardly broken the skin, just pushed the back of his head in.

'I was quite calm now. I had burnt it all out of me at one go, about her, about him, everything. The only thing was, I was sorry for him. Just for those few seconds before he died, when he couldn't see the sense of what I'd done, I'd felt sorry for him, and that was fatal. I didn't know it at the time, but that was where the rot set in. Anyway, I knew at once what I was going to do, and after a bit I did it. I got him up on my shoulder and carried him home. It wasn't easy, of course. They always say it isn't, and it wasn't, but he wasn't a big chap and I managed it. It may seem a fool thing to do, but it wasn't, all that. It was pitch dark, and there was no one about. There never is, on that road at night. I reckoned if a car came along I should have plenty of time to pitch him into the grass at the side, but nothing did. And it was better than getting my car out.

'Somebody would have seen that, or heard it. I'd have had to use the lights. I got him home and took him straight into the wood. There was that clearing in the middle. It was all grass then. It wasn't even very dark, with the trees opening like that, and after a bit I could see what I was doing. The digging wasn't very hard either. I just kept on at it. I had all night. I put him in and covered him up, and then I went back for the case. I meant to take it away with me and get rid of it somewhere, but I hadn't the nerve. I just pitched it in on top of him and covered it up. Only I hadn't really gone deep enough for that, and it was only just covered. Anyway, I tidied it all up as best I could and left it. I finished well before morning. I waited next day to see what would happen and nothing did. I waited two days, and still nothing happened. Then I packed up and went. I never went into the wood again, not till today. And now you say there's nothing there. Where is it, then?'

He had sat all this time with his eyes on the floor, talking as if he was talking to himself, as in a sense he was. But now he lifted his eyes and stared at Merrow. He said, 'I don't understand, John. I must know. Don't you see? I've got to know.' But Merrow still sat there, silent, watching him and wondering what to say.

XVI

Finally Merrow said, 'Well, I told you. I saw you bringing him back. Quite close, I was, down by the path. I didn't say nothing. I didn't do nothing. I didn't see what I could do, except keep quiet. I just waited, same as you did. I wondered where you'd put him, of course. Then Amy told me you were going. I didn't think you'd take him with you, but I looked in the car to make sure, just before you went, and he wasn't in the house, obviously. So I reckoned there was only one place you could have put him, and as soon as you'd gone, I went and looked, and there it was, bloody obvious, to me or anyone else that looked. And they might have, don't you see? If it had once been known something had happened to him, with you going on the way you had been, and then going off like that, they'd have been bound to wonder, and that was one of the first places they'd have looked.

'Only the thing is, no one did know. That was his doing, don't you see? Clever Jack. He was going to do a flit, and he'd collected all he could get and covered all his tracks and sold his car. I suppose he was going to walk to the railway that night. That would have been all right. The police weren't after him, after all. He could have been God knows where before anyone thought of asking. But the only place he got to was your bit of wood, and no one looked for him, even there. But I couldn't know that, and I didn't want him found, any more than you did, or not much. I was all for having him out of the way, but I didn't want you in trouble over it, and all the fuss there'd be. So I reckoned I'd put him where nobody would ever find him, and I had my own ideas about that. It wasn't a job I fancied, I tell you straight, but I'd been in the war, and I knew what I'd need and what to do.

'And then the first thing I found was his suitcase, only just under. Crazy, like I said. But it made me think. I knew then what he'd been up to. I'd known he was going, of course. We all did, only we didn't know when exactly. But when I found the suitcase, I knew he'd been on his way, and I knew then we'd a chance of getting away with it. Anyway, I did what I said. I took my time and made my plans, not like you. I put him where no one will ever find him, and I'm not telling you where, nor anyone else. The suitcase I burnt, and the stuff in it, except the money. Two hundred and forty quid he had in it, and I wasn't going to burn money that somebody could do with. I expect he had some on him, too, but I wasn't going looking for that. The last thing I did was put some young trees in the ground, partly to cover it up, partly to account for the digging, in case anyone looked. Only, as I say, no one ever did, or not as far as I know. So there it is. Five years ago, now, it is, and no one can prove anything.'

He stopped and looked at Hurst, and suddenly smiled. 'Not even you,' he said. 'You could try, of course, if you're dead set on it. My guess is they wouldn't believe you. Even if they did, you couldn't get yourself convicted and punished, if that's what you're after. You and Mr. Richards. Not just on your say-so, and there's nothing else. But you'd have told the whole story by then, just as you've told me, and it wouldn't do Mrs. Richards much good, for a start. Nor me neither. You can see that. I'm not breaking my heart over her, but I like Richards, for all I think he's wrong, and I like myself still more. And there's Lizz, too.' He stopped again. He wasn't smiling any more. He said,

'You can't do it, Mike. You'd better make up your mind to that. I don't even believe you want to, not when you're in your right mind. And that's where we've got to get you.'

He got up. 'Now look,' he said. 'I'm going to cook some breakfast for both of us. We can both do with it. And you're going to go upstairs and unpack. No one knows you're packed except me. I'm not letting you go in your present state, I tell you straight. You go and unpack, and we'll have some breakfast, and then perhaps we can settle something.'

Hurst looked up at him. 'He wasn't Lizz's brother,' he said, 'was he? Not her full brother.'

Merrow smiled and shook his head. 'Not even her half-brother, really, not by nature. She's got plenty of her mother in her. He never had any, not that I could see. He was his father all over again, Jack was, and you can't say worse than that.'

'No, but you can see, can't you? How could I – what could I say to Lizz, with her brother out there in the wood?'

Merrow shrugged. 'I suppose that's right,' he said. 'I don't reckon I'd have let it stop me, not in your place, not with him being the bloody little bastard he was. But I haven't got your niceness. I don't say there's any harm in it. Only one thing or the other. If you're going to feel that way, you shouldn't go killing people, not whatever sort of bastards they are.'

Hurst said, 'If only he hadn't cried like that.'

Merrow stooped over him and took him by the shoulders with his big hands. He lifted him, almost bodily, to his feet and held him there, rocking him slightly too and fro. His face was full of an enormous concern. He said, 'I know. That I can understand. But it wasn't Jack crying like that, not the real grown-up Jack who'd just been making love to that – to your girl. It was some kid that maybe Jack had

149

been once. I don't know, we've all got it in us. But if that was what it was, the kid had been dead long since, and wouldn't never have come back. It was Jack you killed, not the kid. I'd have killed Jack myself if I'd had to, and it wouldn't have worried me no more than a dog I'd killed, and a lot less than some.' He turned Hurst gently and set his face towards the door of the kitchen. 'Anyway,' he said, 'he's not in the wood, is he? He hasn't been, all this time. You've just been imagining it. You go up and look at the trees. You'll see what I mean.'

He moved towards the door, pushing Hurst gently in front of him. Even when they got into the kitchen, Hurst did not say anything. He just turned and went up the stairs, and Merrow turned and went to the cooker and the cupboard where the food was. Up in the bedroom the curtains were still drawn, but there was sunlight behind them. Hurst threw them back and opened the windows. The tops of the trees stood up motionless in the sun. There was the occasional gap in an outline where a branch had gone, but you could not see the destruction on the ground, not from up here. Already the trees were re-making themselves, and had been ever since the wind had dropped, and the dead stuff on the ground was withering, and had been ever since the sun got on to it. The dead leaves would go into the ground and the trees would make new ones, and you could not stop one or the other. It was as if the storm had never happened. For some time he leant on the sill, looking out and listening to the birds. It was the smell of cooking from downstairs that roused him. He pulled himself away from the window and turned guiltily to his cases, and started pulling the things out of them and putting them back in the drawers where they belonged. John was quite right. There was nothing in the wood after all, and hadn't been all this time. Whatever had happened five years ago, the physical link that had chained it to the present was no longer there, and it was sliding away irretrievably into the past. It was the same link that had chained him to the place, and that was broken too. He was free to go away from the place now and stay away from it for ever. It was precisely because he was free to go that he was busy preparing, at least for the moment, to stay.

There was only the mental link left, and that was in his own mind and no one else's. That was what he had to surrender. He had hugged it to him, as Christabel had said, in the way some people hugged their cancers, but now he must give it up. Surrender was the thing. He could see it now. You surrendered to love, other people's love or your own. He doubted if the distinction was a real one. Like John, he did not know much about salvation, but he knew now where it lay. He went on putting his things away with the same automatic precision.

He shut the last drawer, and pushed the empty suitcases under the bed. He was going back to the window when Merrow called him down to breakfast.